Falling Through the Cracks

GWENDOLYN BERNHARD

authorHOUSE®

AuthorHouse™
1663 Liberty Drive
Bloomington, IN 47403
www.authorhouse.com
Phone: 1-800-839-8640

Published by AuthorHouse 2/25/2013

ISBN: 978-1-4817-1866-0 (sc)
ISBN: 978-1-4817-1867-7 (e)

Library of Congress Control Number: 2013903124

SANDRA WALKER, a beautiful, well-groomed, five foot seven widow in her early 50's sits in front of her Doctor at his office. He looks at her with a frown on his face. "I dislike telling you this, but we found a problem with your lungs." What do you mean?" Sandra says in shocked, surprise. "It's an incurable infection called COPD, Chronic Obstructive Lung Disease. Cigarette smokers are the prime target. The symptoms include chronic bronchitis and emphysema. COPD makes breathing difficult. Stop doing what you're doing and add a few years to your life," the Doctor advises. He writes her prescriptions for three inhalants. "I'll call the pharmacy for you, they'll help your breathing. There is no cure for this disease, but living life well is possible." You have to deal with anxiety, breathe more efficiently, use less energy and protect yourself from infections. And quit smoking. Sandra leaves the office close to tears.

In her small immaculate one bedroom apartment, located in Tequesta, a safe, secure, community in South Florida, Sandra sits at the kitchen table and stares at the dark screen of her laptop. She wonders aloud if the disease only infects Afro-Americans, her native heritage. Sitting back in her chair, she scratches her dread locked hair, and listens to classical music. With a sad look on her face, she stubbornly lights a cigarette. Her thoughts wander to the past, a constant habit not easy to ignore.

After a few puffs, she lifts her hands over her head stretches her body and close her eyes. Within seconds, her Cocker-Poodle, Hope, jumps around the chair holding her favorite plush toy in her mouth. She wants to play. Instead, Sandra lovingly shoos her away, folds her hands as if in prayer and thinks of her son's father.

When they met, he was a Staff Sergeant in the Air Force at a base, near her hometown in Michigan. Sandra had just broken up with her first boyfriend, Gary, after a long high school relationship. She was employed as a Long Distance Operator for a state owned telephone Company. Joseph was 28 years old and almost 6 feet tall, a giant of a man to her 19 year old, well-proportioned body. Sandra instantly fell in love with him. This would give her the opportunity to get away from her Mother who constantly put her down. According to her Mother, she would never make anything out of herself. She was sick of hearing these daily negative statements.

The other reason, Sandra wanted to get away was because of her stepfather, who would quietly walk behind her and feel her breasts when she was doing dishes at the kitchen sink. He convinced her that was something that Father's were allowed to do. When she told her Mother in frustration what was happening, she laughed and told her to stop lying. On the other hand, Joseph encouraged her to find a career that would suit her talents. He felt she had more to offer than just being a telephone operator. From the age of 17, She never told anyone how she felt about what was happening to her. Besides Joseph, her closest friend was her dog Blackie.

Joseph asked her to marry him after a year of dating. With their modest income, her parents partially paid for a formal Military wedding. In her trance, she visualized the arguments between her parents about the cost of the wedding. It was a special occasion. She was still a virgin and proud of it. Sandra paid the remaining cost of the wedding and reception with her hard-earned savings. They said their vows at the base chapel. Family and friends attended. Except her older brother, who was in Jackson State Prison for burglary. She also heard from one of his friends that he was hooked on heroin. Instead of these negative thoughts, she envisioned her beautiful white wedding dress with a long silk and lace train.

A year later, Sandra had a healthy; 8-pound son that the happy couple promptly named Joseph Junior. Shortly after, Joseph transferred to Northern California. As soon as, they settled into an off base apartment, Joseph ended up deployed to Vietnam for a one-year tour of duty. Sandra and the baby left to fend for themselves. On the first of every month, Sandra ran to the mailbox to garner her meager, government housing check from Joseph.

To help make ends meet, she worked as a Hostess at a trendy beachside restaurant. With her vibrant personality, and good looks, she actually attracted more business. Frequent dinner guests, who had become friends, came every weekend just to see how she was doing with Joey Junior by having to live on her own. They also gave her large tips, whether they got the best table or not. This admiration led her to believe that she could work in marketing and sales. She worked for a short time on the phone for a telemarketing company. Their main business goal was to sell time-share vacations in the Bahamas. Immediately, she earned her hard won commission and weekly salary.

When Joseph returned from Vietnam, he was a very different man. They argued constantly especially when he smoked marijuana. He also suffered from nightmares, anxiety, sleepless nights, and Post-Traumatic Stress Disorder, commonly known as PTSD. Sandra kept her day job but smoked with him to help him change to a mellow mood. She quickly became addicted to the substance. Within three years, Joseph had an early release from the Military due to cutbacks at the end of the Vietnam War. He stayed at home complaining to Sandra about hearing voices. During these nightly interludes, along with sexual trauma, Sandra's coping skills became nil. To make matters worse, Joseph junior always cried in the background. After eight years of marriage, they divorced.

Sandra came to her senses after hearing a loud knock on the door. "Who is it?" she yells. A. muffled reply comes from the other side of the door, "its Peggy." Sandra opens the door with a smile. "Hey Girlfriend, come on in." Barking incessantly, Hope jumps around Peggy's feet. She bends down showing a fair amount of suntanned cleavage. Her blonde curls frame her face. She rubs Hope's head, "you miss me baby, you miss me," she gushes. Hope shakes her head from side to side and runs to her kennel.

Peggy turns her attention to Sandra, "Its time for you and me to go out and have some fun." Laughing, Sandra remarks, "With the way you look in those skin tight leggings, stiletto heels and that v-neck shirt without a bra, no one will pay attention to me. When you were petting Hope, she looked like she wanted to breast feed." "Oh, come on girl, you know as well I do that you'll have a debt free evening, cause the men at the bar will want to buy you drinks," Peggy lamented. " "Besides that, it's the season. All those folks from up North are flowing into Florida right now." "You keep forgetting that I don't drink anymore," Sandra wails. "Right, but I do. Let's go to the *Hideaway*." I need a couple of bottles of that new drink vodka ice in my system. Come on, it's Friday, cocktail hour." "Okay, you've convinced me. I will go and drink my ginger ale. Keep in mind; nothing will get in the way of my sobriety." And I need to go too the drug store to pick up prescriptions." "No problem let's go."

Peggy drove her compact car to a parking space in front of the *Hideaway*, an upscale, neighborhood, bar and grille, supported by local residents. When the duo walks in, the bar, the clientele greets them with a round of applause. Sandra wears a short leather skirt plus a buttoned down leather vest. Topping off her sexy attire are high heel shoes. Peggy whispers to Sandra as they head to the crowded bar, "you see we're still the salt and pepper queens of Palm Beach County." Sandra smiles.

As soon as they sit down, the Owner/ Bartender, Nick, places a small plastic cup in front of each of them. "Whenever you're ready Ladies, the drinks are on Angelo." "I bet he loves buying ginger ale.

It only costs a dollar." Sandra chuckled "Where does that holier than thou attitude come from?" Peggy says sharply. "I just want my best friend to quit, drinking," Sandra muses. "Why don't you play the jukebox while I visit with Angelo?" Peggy asserts. Looking around the bar and at the pool table, where four white guys are shooting pool. One wears a cowboy hat, tight jeans a denim shirt and expensive boots. Sandra realizes that once again, she is the only person of color in attendance. "These people don't want to hear my kind of music," she retorts "Go ahead, play some Motown," Peggy smirks. "These guys need a change from Country and Western." "Maybe I need a change. With or without you I'm here three or four times a week." Sandra shoots back. She angrily slides off her bar stool and walks to the jukebox. Browsing through the selections, made her think hard and steadfast about the past.

After pressing, the button of a rhythm and blues song, the music starts playing; her body sways from side to side. Overall, Sandra plays twenty songs. She goes back to the bar. Peggy is so engrossed with Angelo she did not even notice her. Sandra picks up a refill of ginger ale and moves to an empty booth. Humming to the current song blaring through the speakers, she glances out the window at the starlit night sky, and smiles.

Sandra's thoughts flash to her second marriage to Monty, a moderately, wealthy, Jewish man well known in the whole sell clothing business. She reminisces about them working together at their large showroom in San Francisco. During the four seasons, she modeled the clothing when they met with buyers from large, retail stores and outlets. They lived in Marin County a well-to-do enclave outside of San Francisco. As she flicked her upper lip, her memories carry her further into the past. Their three bedrooms home was complete with swimming pool, a view of the Golden Gate Bridge and the Bay area. The property was valued at $500,000.00, not bad for a girl from East Detroit, Michigan.

Joseph Jr. was eight years old when Sandra met Monty. She was so proud of him. He was very handsome and the spitting image of his father. Joey did not relate to Monty, he kept asking when his father was going to take him away from that man. There was never an answer. All Sandra could do was shake her head, and pour herself a glass of wine. In fact, when she was alone there was no problem for her to drink a bottle of Merlot wine and quickly smoke a pricey pack of Sherman Cigarettelos throughout the afternoon. This habit came about, from having an unhappy, bored life. The only excitement Monty had at the end of every week was to light the candle while he said his prayers in his Jewish language. Out of her weaning love for him, she learned the Friday night prayers and begin to light the candle herself.

During the eve of their sixth wedding anniversary, Sandra made another big decision in her life. She decided to divorce Monty and move to Hollywood. Her conviction was that a modeling career could take off. Maybe she would become a famous model and or an actor. After her years with Monty, she certainly knew the ropes of the business. Her excitement about this new mission made her tremble. Joey was not happy with this venture. He said he was scared to move. He would miss his friends at school. He also changed his mind about living with Monty. Sandra explained that it was an adventure and they would have a good time. In addition, even though Monty did not like her plan, he gave her several thousand dollars to get started. What a great surprise. This made her feel stronger about her move to Southern California.

Peggy yelled at her from the bar, "Sandra, come on over here, Girl. You're missing out on all the fun." "I'm busy right now," she retorted. Another song begins playing prompting Sandra to start dancing by herself near one of the pool tables. Peggy sashays over to Sandra and dances with her. Their exotic moves motivate people at the two patron deep bar to dance around them. Including, a homeless man nicknamed Willie. He is shirtless and dressed in tattered shorts, a vest, and dirty flip flop sandals. To top off his look, he has matted hair. The regulars accept him because he used to be in the advertising business. He is known as an intelligent man and wishes to live the way he does. He even has his own cell phone. Nor, does he accept or ask for handouts. Outside, is his shopping cart filled with his belongings. His two dogs wait for him on the sidewalk by the door.

When the song finishes Willie bows and says, "Thank you ladies," He rolls a cigarette and goes outside. Sandra wobbles back to the booth exhausted. Peggy walks beside her. "I'm tired," Sandra says as she tries to catch her breath. "You want me to take you home?" asks Peggy. Sandra sadly nods her head as she lights a cigarette. "And I haven't even heard all the songs," Sandra proclaims.

"But more important, there's something, I want to talk to you about, news from my Doctor." "Okay, we'll go to your apartment have some coffee, and talk," Peggy states. Sandra nods. They leave the *Hideaway* followed by the moans of near drunken men at the bar. Peggy shouts over the music, "I'll be back." They get in the car and drive away. In the car, they smile at each other in triumph. "It didn't take long to get my three Friday night drinks," Peggy slurs. "And free, "says Sandra. It starts to rain as Peggy drives Sandra home.

"Here we go, one of our tropical storms," asserts Peggy. "You know it won't last long, just another five minute Florida down pour." Sandra says with impatience. "Why does it have to happen in the dark of night, "Only God can tell you that?" Peggy offers. "You're right", Sandra says with pouty lips. "So turn on the music and put some soul in the car." Peggy turns the radio knob back and forth while Sandra lights a cigarette. When Sandra looks up, she sees a pair of headlights speeding in their direction. A pick up trunk hits them head on. A religious song plays in the background.

Sandra lays unconscious in a hospital Intensive Care Unit. Her head is wrapped in bandages, there is an oxygen Hose in her nose and IV's are bandaged on both arms. Cards and flowers along with a few stuffed animals and balloons overflow the room. A Nurse takes her pulse. Standing near by is an Intern. The Nurse finishes her work and turns to the Intern. "This lady is very lucky. The Doctors think she will make it. The Driver of the car was not so fortunate. Nor was the person in the truck. He died at the scene." The Nurse orders the Intern to keep a close check on Sandra when she does her rounds. The Nurse and Intern leave the room.

Sandra's mind gravities to life with her third husband Eugene and her now teenage son Joey. Eugene was the Creator of a famous mascot for an international restaurant chain. He also published a fun and activity book for the children of families who dined at the popular eateries. She met Eugene when she won a role as a Prostitute in an independent film he co-produced. Their first meeting was at the Cast party and film preview, held on a 135 feet Fed ship yacht owned by a couple who invested in the movie. She introduced herself and said, "I loved performing in your film. I hope I get to work with you again." He smiled at her and took her hand.

"You are not going to work for me you are going to work with me because I am going to marry you." Sandra laughed, "Is this a joke?" "No I'm serious I want you to be my ninth wife." "Why have you been married so many times?" "This is not the place to discuss my German heritage or my history with women. Let us just say I was practicing until I got to you." Sandra chuckled; "You certainly have a great sense of humor, and incredible honesty." "Does that come with your German heritage?" Sandra asked. "There is no reason to lie. Life is to short for that," Eugene smiled. "Keep in mind I'm about 20 years older than you.

So, beware of what I say." "You're not going anywhere soon," Sandra quips.

Six weeks later, Eugene and Sandra were married in Las Vegas at the Little Chapel of the West. Joey served as Best Man. The wedding was elegant and simple. Sandra was happier than ever. Even though Eugene had three adult children and a younger brother, none of them chose to attend. There were no guests.

Their palatial million-dollar home in Beverly Hills, surrounded by celebrity neighbors, was complete with a lighted tennis court and swimming pool. Their Spanish live- in housekeeper, had her own quarters with a private entrance. In fact, they were the only resident's on the avenue with a tennis court. As a wedding gift, Eugene, had a silver Mercedes coupe delivered to their brick driveway behind double wooden gates. After all, Eugene had a 3.5 Mercedes and a classic Rolls Royce. No reason Sandra should not have an up to date, classic, car of her own. The advertising and sales office housed in a historic Spanish building in downtown Los Angeles was equally as stylish. Eugene appointed Sandra as Executive Vice President of the agency, Ivory Advertising Corporation. The Artist for client jobs, the company Accountant and the Printing Company all worked off -premises. Sandra's mission was to gather new marketing customers by telephone. At the beginning she had, a hard time convincing would be clients. Eugene finally wrote her a script to read. Dressed in a business suit, we see her smoking a cigarette, listening to music and pitching her story.

In a few months, Sandra had three companies signed for the agency advertising and marketing plan. She and Eugene celebrate her victory with champagne at their private club, *Check Mate* in Beverly Hills. The décor of the club is British. Mahogany walls, crystal chandeliers, and a dark lit Game Room with prim and proper tables and chairs surrounding a large extravagant tank filled with tropical fish. There formal dining room walls are covered with artwork by famous and local Artists. Outside the informal dining area, Sandra and Eugene sit at a lead glass table with an umbrella overhead. Smooth playing music is in the background.

The next step Eugene proclaimed was to enroll Joey in the Carlton Academy, one of the most sought after high schools in the area, with a long waiting list. Hugging Eugene with appreciation, Sandra cried,

"You're the best husband I could ever have. I can't wait to tell Joey." "He earned it with his good grades, and with a little help from my friends," Eugene smiles. "Well, you might as well get use to it; there will not be a tenth wife." Oh, I know that." Don't want one." He holds the ring finger of her left hand, "why do you think I gave you a three carat ring when I asked you to marry me?" "I don't know, but I'm learning more everyday." A romantic song begins to play. Sandra stands up and holds out her hands, "Let's dance, my knight in shining armor." Eugene takes her in his arms. They slither on to the dance floor. After the dance, they head home for a night of bountiful lovemaking.

During the morning after two male neighbors are playing tennis. Sandra sits on the sidelines secretly smoking a joint under a large palm tree. The older man, Theodore, throws up his hands in exhaustion, "That's it for me." He turns towards Sandra. "I have something that I think you'll like. Come on over to our house. Once inside the new age furnished home, the three some sit next to each other.

Robin the younger man takes out a small plastic bag full of white nuggets. "What's that?" Sandra asks. "It's called crack," Randy offers. "What does it do?" "It's made from cocaine, be patient we'll show you how to use it in a minute." Theodore takes a glass pipe with gold screens from a box on the table. Randy pours a shot of 151 Rum into a glass and dips cotton wrapped scissors into it. Randy drops a piece of the cocaine into the pipe. He lights the cotton, takes a puff and passes it to Sandra. She takes a puff. "Oh wow," she exclaims. "I have to tell Eugene about this." "You probably shouldn't, I don't want him to keep us from playing tennis on your court, or from having you as our friend."

Isn't cocaine very expensive?" Yes, between the two of us, we spend close to a thousand dollars a week. "Come on that's impossible. How do you live like this and spend that kind of money?" Sandra quizzes. "Don't forget my inheritance," Theodore interjects."You are right, I forgot. So give me another hit." Sandra continued to experience a euphoria she had never felt before.

As time went on, she lost a lot of weight by privately chasing her high. She had to adjust to her low periods when working at the agency. The best advantage to her addiction was that Eugene did not have a clue to what she was doing. However, Joey sensed something was wrong, "Mom, why do you act so different?" He would ask from time to time.

Her answer would always be that she was trying to lose 10 pounds. "Must be the diet pills," she said sorrowfully.

During her unconscious state of mind, Sandra remembers more about her life. Like the time, she became a sought after local model. There were also articles about her in prominent newspapers and magazines. One article, in a national magazine on *How to Be Successful in the Worlds of Glamour and Business,* was critically acclaimed. She also created a cartoon talk show for kids, televised by a national TV station, which specialized in children's programming. The Saturday morning one hour, show lasted 3 seasons. At the same time, she served as President of a television and motion picture association. Her resume was so impressive that she was either too old or over qualified for different local modeling assignments. In addition, agencies were becoming more interested in girls in their late teens and early twenties.

Sandra had a team of Dealers at her disposal. She would buy several grams of powder cocaine at a time. Cook it in a tablespoon filled with a small portion of water. Then put the spoon on top of a lighted candle. Once the powder liquefied, she put the spoon on a bowl filled with ice cubes. Most of the time, Sandra could not wait for her first hit. Before she knew what was happening, her supply would be gone. Then she turned to drinking wine and taking pills. Her symptoms took a change for the worse. She had paranoia and started to do her hits in the bedroom closet. Nor would she share her stash. After a while Sandra begin to think of her craziness. She realized she needed help but refused to get it. After all, COPD is an incurable disease. Moreover, it became clear that so is drug and pill addiction.

Almost every evening, at the Hollywood Hills home of a successful, Attorney she was sitting at a round table of well-to-do professionals, passing a crack pipe to each other. Each person smoked his or her own stash. It was the company of others that put them together. They all smoked marijuana before leaving the premises. Sandra enjoyed these secret evening jaunts because she felt like an equal and she was meeting important people. This went on for almost four years. Eugene had misgivings about her behavior. However, overall, she kept him happy in their 4-poster king size canopy bed and was a perfect Hostess to their clients.

She was the talk of the town during Holidays and other special events. Slowly, Joey distanced himself from Sandra and drew closer to his father, who lived in Northern California. When he graduated from Carlton Academy, all at Eugene's expense, he had his choice of universities to attend. He chose a prestigious school, in Massachusetts, which offered him a scholarship. When Joey graduated from college, he called Sandra to tell her he was not coming home. He was in love and was getting married in his new love's hometown in upstate New York. Sandra had not even met her Daughter-In-Law to be, nor was she or Eugene invited to the wedding.

Eugene decided that he wanted to move from Southern California to New England to be closer to his oldest son, Jonathon and stepson Joey. He decided to find a large enough property to house a home office environment. Luckily, due to modern technology, he was able to keep his current clients and add more from the East coast. The move was very profitable. Their center chimney colonial riverside five-bedroom home, sat on 100 acres of land by a river. The house in California is to be kept vacant. The worse thing about the new environment was the cold, spine, tingling, winters. Eugene and Sandra endured homebound heavy snowstorms. This happened so often that Sandra gave up all her vices except alcohol and cigarettes. In addition, her other vices were too hard to get in the small village where they lived.

Eugene announced on one of those snowy evenings, while sitting at the dinner table that they were going to go on a vacation to Mexico, his favorite stomping ground. When she heard the news, Sandra was astonished. He went on to tell her that the first journey would be to Cancun. "I want to make you happy for the rest of my life," he swooned. How could I not be happy, I have never been to Mexico, not even out of the USA? Do we need passports?" "No. I just need you by my side in your bikini," Eugene teased." "From Cancun we are going to Cozumel and then on to Acapulco," Eugene smiled. "This is my 16th anniversary gift to you, darling." Well, I have a present for you, Sandra says. As she jiggles her breasts up and down, moves her tongue around her lips and dances around him as she throws her dress on the floor. You know you're my KISA, knight in shining armor," Eugene rises from the table and takes off his pants, while Sandra kneels before him on her knees.

In Acapulco, they stayed at the plush Via Vera resort where they were treated like royalty. Sandra fell in love with the white sand beaches and Margarita's. Sitting on the beach under a large umbrella, she guzzled one margarita after another, while Eugene swam with the fish in the ocean. Soon, Sandra became bored. She pleaded with Eugene to find them other ways of excitement. There were too many tourists in Acapulco and she could not even speak Spanish. They returned home after two weeks instead of six.

The day of their arrival home, Sandra received a call from an old friend. "Hey lady, this is Monique, I'm in town. Hope I can see you and Eugene. You know I especially want to see you," said the excited, flirty voice. Sure, come on over," Sandra responded. Later that evening, Monique, a tall, elegant, black fashion model with red hair shows up at the front door. The women hug and kiss. You're still the sexist woman I know,'" gushes Monique. Well, you're not too bad yourself." "Nope we haven't aged a bit," claims Sandra. They walk into the sunken living room and sit down on the velvet sofa. "Where's Eugene?" "He's in bed. We had a long trip home. What's with the red hair?" Sandra asks. "I had to dye my hair for a photo session in Hawaii," Monique answers.

Sandra gets up and heads for the bedroom. "Okay, let us see what my man is doing." Eugene is asleep. Monique sits on the king size bed and kisses him on the cheek. He pulls her into his arms. "Hold old boyfriend, it's me Monique." Eugene opens his eyes in surprise, "Where'd you come from?" "Just got into town and immediately came to see you and Sandra." Let's have some fun," Monique goes on. I have an idea let us put Sandra in the middle and make love to her." "That is something new and different," says Eugene as he looks lovingly at Sandra. "You mean after all these years of marriage, you've never tried it?" "Never thought of it," Sandra answers. "Besides, I don't think you do that with just anybody."

Monique takes off her clothes. Sandra unrobes then sits on the middle of the bed. Eugene moves to one side of her. Monique lies down on the other side. Sandra stretches out and closes her eyes. Eugene and Monique stroke Sandra's body and kiss her nipples. Sandra moans in appreciation. Eugene gets on top of her while Monique massages his back. The trio takes passion to the nigh degree by centering their attention on Sandra. Each of them climax together. They fall back on the bed smiling and laughing. "You both sure give great love," Sandra gushes. "Now you know what a *ménage a trios* is," Monique says

breathlessly. "I will see you kids soon, I am off to a photo shoot in New York and I am already late. Many thanks, to each of you." She blows a kiss, dresses, gather her belongings and rush out.

Sandra's mind flashes to the scene when she was driving her Mercedes with the top down on a hot, breezy, summer day to meet Jonathon at his clothing store in a ritzy Massachusetts, suburb. She pulls her Mercedes up to the trendy boutique and gets out. The people on the street look at her as if she had stolen the car. She laughs to herself and glides into the store. "Look who's here," Jonathon expresses. "What do I owe the pleasure?" "I need to ask a small favor," "Anything for you Babe," Jonathon says as he gives Sandra a bear hug. "I can't share my request now, you've got customers. Take care of them first. I'll go outside and smoke a cigarette."

Jonathon joins Sandra. "How's Dad?" he asks. "He's fine," she answers. "Look, I'll go straight to the point, I've been clean for almost a year." Sandra says. "And now you want to relapse, right?" "I wouldn't call it that. A small amount of Pot would be just fine." "The answer is NO," Jonathon says sternly. "Oh, come on just this one time." "NO," Jonathon yells. "Okay, okay it was nice to see you," Sandra quips. She gets in the car and quickly drives off. "What a wimp," she mutters.

At home, Sandra finds Eugene visiting with his long time friend Thomas who has just arrived from Canada. "You know I was just telling Eugene, that you and he should visit Florida." Thomas offers. "Man if you like it, you know I'll like it. There's no reason to live like this most of the year," Eugene asserts. You are right." Sandra interjects. "How do you think I feel, putting up with the winters in Vancouver?" Thomas adds.

Sandra goes on to visualize their first trip to Palm Beach. The couple registers at a historic hotel on the main street of the island. The man at the front desk thinks Sandra is Eugene's Caregiver. "Sir, would you like separate quarters for the lady?" "No, Eugene says sharply. The lady is my wife." "I'm sorry Sir; I didn't mean to cause a misunderstanding." Eugene grabs the room key and stalks away. With a sneer on her face, Sandra follows. She desperately wanted to give the Desk Clerk the finger.

After a few weeks, Sandra wakes up from her coma. Most of the dressings are removed from her head. The dread locks are gone. Her

straight, short-cropped hair is combed flat to her scalp. She awakens when two old friends from the *Hideaway*, Gina, a well-preserved brown-haired lady in her 60's and Ralph her balding spouse, come to visit. "Where am I?" she feebly asks. You are in the hospital, Gina replies. "Where's Peggy?" Gina and Ralph sorrowfully look at each other.

"You were in a car accident. Peggy didn't make it," Ralph whispers as he strokes her hand. Sandra moans. A Nurse comes into the room. "I think you better go," she says to Gina and Ralph. "I have to give her medication to control the trauma." The duo leave and the Nurse administer a tranquilizer in Sandra's arm. Sandra floats back into another trance.

She sees her and Eugene standing on the balcony of their Florida condominium on the Intracoastal, looking at the view. They are holding hands. "Well, Sweetheart Sandra says, I need to go to the newspaper office to edit my column." "By all means, I'm very proud of your success in getting the job in such a short period of time." "I didn't want you to think that I couldn't work with you, Sandra responses" "On the contrary, your true talents are showing you what you can do best," replies Eugene. "I hope you feel better," Sandra states.

"I'll take a nap while you're gone. Do not forget Thomas is coming to town. "Yeah, and here it's raining while the sun shines. We definitely live in the Tropics," Sandra remarks. "We have a reservation for dinner with him at *Who Done It*," Eugene says sternly."And we can't get there to late or we'll have to wait an hour to be seated," Sandra smiles. "You got it, Darling," Eugene prompts. Sandra kisses him on the cheek "When I get back, we'll talk about selling the house back East and make this our permanent home" She says and walks out.

As Sandra maneuvers her Mercedes in traffic, with the radio blaring jazz music, she receives a call on her car phone. "This is Thomas, the caller said. You should go home Eugene has had a heart attack. He died on the way to the hospital." Sandra is so befuddled she rear ends the car in front of her at an intersection. She turns off the radio. The Police arrive quickly. Sandra talks to the Policeman about her dilemma. The aging Driver of the other car could care less. "At least give the bitch a ticket," he asserts. Sandra begins crying. The Policeman tries to calm both of them down.

He asks to see her driver's license. She cannot find it. "Don't you

understand? I just got a call that my husband died from a heart attack," she wailed. ""She probably stole the car" the other driver, quips. Sandra goes on, "I don't live that far away. Please, give me a ride home and I'll show you my license." Do you at least have the registration of the car?" the Policeman asks. Sandra looks in the glove compartment and gives the Policeman the registration. "Okay. Mrs. Walker, I understand your situation. I'll take you home but, I still have to give you a ticket." "Where do you want your car towed?" "I don't know, I've never had anything like this happen to me," Sandra cries.

When Sandra arrives home, she shows the Policeman her driver's license. When he leaves, she immediately downs a glass of wine and smokes a cigarette. She calls Joey to tell him the news. There is no answer. She has not talked to him in over a year. He never returns her calls. She was baffled at his lack of respect. She tearfully leaves a message. "Sweetheart, call me. Papa Eugene has died from a heart attack." Then she calls Thomas. Where are you?" she asks."I am in my suite at the Astor Lake Hotel. Do you need me?" "Of course I do. I can't handle this by myself." "I'll be right over, Thomas replies. Sandra hangs up the phone and collapses in to tears as she reaches for the bottle of wine. She puts a few pills in her mouth and gulps down a drink from the bottle.

Thomas arrived a short time later and finds Sandra totally drunk and incoherent. He makes a pot of coffee and reassures her that he is her friend and will stick by her side during this ordeal. Within a week, Eugene's Attorney reads the Will to Sandra, "Eugene wants to be cremated". The Urn would be transported to Berlin, Germany by his son Jonathon. This was a shocking surprise to Sandra mainly because Eugene never discussed death or cremation. With Thomas' help, she stayed sober and followed through with the requested details. Thomas reassures her again that he is a true friend and wraps Eugene's polo sweater around her shoulders. Sandra continues to vacillate in her flashback.

After Eugene's death in 2007, the biggest surprise was that he left a small bequest to each of his other eight wives. Sandra was outraged. How could he do this to her, She wondered. After all, she had been married to him the longest, over 17 years, and was his most devoted wife. The Attorney was not much assistance; he said the Will was iron clad. It made no difference to what he said. Sandra threatened to find another Attorney and fight the Will. The Attorney told her to go ahead with her plans. He had been Eugene's Attorney, not hers. He reminded her, that she was to receive a large sum of money, including her car, which was only partially paid for and the condominium, where she would still have to take care of monthly expenses."What about our home in Massachusetts?" she asked. He told her that it was a rental property. He also told her that advertising agency is to in her name. He advised her that if she did not notify the clients, the company would fall into negative revenue balances. Sandra was devastated with all this news in one meeting. However, at least, she was to get the furniture in both residences. This Includes to the company clients. Nevertheless, what would she do with them?

As the weeks pass, Sandra's drug and alcohol abuse become worse. First, she lost the Mercedes due to lack of payments and started taking the bus, which she hated. Every time she got on a crowded bus, she thought she was in another country. Spanish and Haitian people were speaking so loud in their natives' language, it was hard to hear the bus stop announcements. Some how, she continued to write her weekly column *Quick Takes* for the newspaper and stayed in touch with ad clients by phone, but little else. She had put the agency clients on hold. Told them that in Eugene's memory the company would be closed for a while. All her free time was spent hiding in another world because of her addictions. She did come to her senses, found a used Kia and bought it with the last of her savings. The rest of the money slowly fizzled down to a few hundred dollars.

Within months, Sandra had spent all her money from excessive drug use, was forced to pawn her wedding ring and a diamond necklace in order to buy groceries in order to live. She even applied for food stamps. She is turned-downed because she made too much money. This forced her to go to shelters and get grocery handouts as if she was homeless. This weighed heavy on her self-esteem and dignity. Sandra becomes accepted by the Health Care District. She felt more comfortable with herself knowing that if she needed medical attention for her COPD she could see a Doctor without charge.

.About three months after Eugene's death, Sandra, was served a Foreclosure Notice on the condomimiun. It was too costly to maintain.

She called Joey, who was now the father of a baby girl. He had sent her a photo album of pictures of the baby. Because of the selfishness of her habits, Sandra did not respond to Joey and his wife, Dina, about the pictures. They still lived in upstate New York and she was in Florida. Again, she heard his answering machine message. "Joey, please call me. I am sorry I have not been in touch with you. Times are hard. I really need to talk to you," she said close to tears.

Sandra hangs up the phone and begins to cry. What's wrong with him," I will always be his Mother. I did not raise him to be the person he has become. On, the other hand, I have not been the kind of Mother he thought I was. "There's a dark cloud over us." She composed herself and called Monique. No answer, she leaves a message. "Monique, I want to talk to you my friend." "It's time to get the Devil off my ass." Disgusted, she throws the phone on the table.

Sandra's eyes blink as a Nurse takes her blood pressure. "How are you Ms. Walker,?" The Nurse asks. "Miserable." Sandra hiccups. "How long have I been here?" "This is your third week. From the looks of things you'll be going home in another week." "Not too soon for me. Can I have a mirror to see what I look like?" Sandra asks. "I wouldn't want to do that right now," the Nurse advises. "By the way," the Nurse goes on, she takes out a notebook.

"Your friend Monique is taking care of your dog," And she also has the rest of your personal effects from a Lewis Clark." "Thank God for that Hope is my best friend. Certainly not Lewis, "Sandra grumbles. "And your friends Gina and Ralph have checked on your apartment." "And, I understand your car is safe." "That's good." "Well, relax and here take this," the Nurse gives her a pill cup. "It will help you with your pain." "Is it a narcotic?" "Unfortunately, it is." "Good." Sandra smiles and swallows the pill. "Good night," the Nurse says. "Thank you Nurse. You're an Angel."

Within minutes, Sandra is back into her trance like state of mind. She remembers when she was foreclosed on her condominium with 30 days to find a place to live. She put her furniture in storage and slept in the back seat of the Kia in the parking lot of a 24-hour discount store. In the mornings, she would discreetly go into the restroom of the store and freshen up. During one of these surreys, she met Lewis, a tall man in his late 30's, who worked the night shift at the store. He asked her out for breakfast at a Diner. She agreed. They became fast friends.

He asked her where she lived, she told him the truth. "I'm living in my car until I can find an apartment I can afford," she said nonchalantly "You can't do that . "I have a two-bedroom apartment come and stay with me. I won't charge you much and I need a roommate" I don't even know your name," "Sorry, Lewis Clark. And you are?" "Sandra Walker" she replies. "Every morning when I get off from work I see you and your car. First I thought you worked here." "Thanks for not reporting me to the management." "I wouldn't do that," he smiles. Sandra smiles back, and says yes to his offer. They look at each other in anticipation.

Their relationship was hot and heavy. They had so many daily sexual encounters that Sandra never saw the second bedroom. The lovemaking was intense. Lewis was so engrossed with her that his large penis was hard from the moment he touched her. He loved licking her body and she loved licking and sucking him. This went on for the next six months. It was convenient for Sandra because Lewis's apartment was only a block away from the newspaper office. Lewis did not take pills or drugs, so when he was at work, Sandra smoked crack with her friends, some time in the morning, she would get home minutes before him. Within months, Sandra saw a personality defect in Lewis that made her uncomfortable. He was possessive. If she was not leaning over her laptop working on her newspaper column, Lewis would demand to see what she had written. Most of the time she had only a few paragraphs. Not enough for him. She would calm him down by bringing home a six -pack of beer, play sexy music and do a strip tease.

One early morning, on her way home, to Lewis, Sandra was stopped in the driveway by a Policeman for speeding. Home from work early, Lewis stood at their front door shaking his head. The Policeman asks to see her license and registration. When she opens her glove box, a new crack stem falls on the floor. The Policeman sees it, and picks it up. "Get out of the car, he orders and put your hands behind your back." He handcuffs Sandra. "What have I done?" Sandra asks.

"Lady, you're driving around with paraphernalia I'm having your car towed, and taking you to the county jail." "What?" Sandra, screams as she puts her hands behind her back. "You heard me." He helps her get in his car. He gets in the driver's seat and speeds away. That evening,

Monique bails her out of jail. During 90 days, she wrote her weekly column, took two or three buses a day to get to her destinations and waited for her court date. When she stood before the Judge, he took her license away for 5 years. After, 9 months her relationship with Lewis ended. Even though he had loving feelings for her, he could not accept her drug habits. He never even smoked cigarettes let alone pot and crack. He helped her find the apartment she currently lives in. It is close to a Park and a local bus stop.

Monique enters the hospital room carrying a stuffed animal and kisses Sandra's cheek. Sandra wakes up and reaches out her hand. "Hello my Darling," Monique whispers. Oh, I am so glad you are here. How's Hope?" "Happy to be with me but misses you. She has learned how to use the puppy pad and is not making messes on the floor. I let her sleep in my bed, just like you do." "I love you for taking care of her. Besides you, she's my best friend," Sandra offers. "I know," Monique says tearfully.

After 3 weeks, Sandra is released from the hospital. She sits outside the main entrance in a wheel chair, waiting for Monique to pick her up. A muscular, man passes her smoking a cigarette. She politely asks if she can buy a cigarette from him. "As beautiful as you are I'll give you the pack, lady." Sandra sports a wide grin, showing her perfect white teeth. "One will do me just fine. I have to stop smoking any way." "So do I, he says with a toothless grin. Are you married?" he asks." I' am a widow. What's your name?" "Sandra Walker." "I'm Spencer Madison. Nice to meet you." "You too. What do you do for a living, Spencer?". "I'm retired." "Huh, you look to young to be retired. I am 50, but lucky for me I had early retirement. I was hurt on the job. But, I have a job on the side." Monique, drives up. "Here's my ride." Nice to meet you." "I have a feeling we'll meet again." Spencer says as he helps Sandra in to the car.

Monique and Sandra hug. Hope stands on the back seat barking and wagging her tail. "You smell like cigarette smoke. Have you started all ready?" "Could not wait. You're going to kill yourself." "Maybe that is what I need to do. Joey never returned my calls during the 3 weeks I was in the hospital. I left messages that I was in the hospital from a car accident and that I have COPD. He's all the family I have." "Stop feeling sorry for yourself." "When Joey's ready to call, he will." "But, you don't understand the last time I talked to him, he said his Mother was dead." "How can he not love you? You are still his mother. Without you and his father he would not be on this earth." "All right, I won't put my miseries on you," Sandra whines."Take me to the drug store I need to pick up a few prescriptions." Yes, your Highness." Monique teases. "And don't forget I'm your family."

Sandra walks in to her apartment. Her phone rings. "Hello, yes I'm home and I can write the column this week. No, I will not let you down. I will write about riding the bus. It's such a different experience for me." Is that okay?" Thank you so much. I will get the draft into the office before deadline. Thanks again for believing in me". She walks to the table and sits in front of her laptop. Hope lays down besides the chair. Sandra stares at the screen then gets up, goes to a kitchen cabinet takes out a bottle of wine and half fills a glass. She takes a pill and washes it down with the wine. Then turns the radio on to her favorite easy listening station. With sheer determination, Sandra starts typing. Smiling, she stops and lights a cigarette. Okay, she says out loud looking at Hope. "She lowers her head in prayer then begins writing in earnest. She spews out her sentences as she types.

I have to tell you that one of the reasons I like riding the bus, is the friendliness of the Drivers. That is most of them. Several Drivers I have known in the last year have become friends. Highly unlikely in most major cities especially where there is a lot of hustle and bustle. At least I think so. Since I live alone, I look forward to daily bus trips to the office and here and there. Basically, for one simple fact, I can fantasize about who the Driver will be. However, on one particular day I was surprised to no end.

The Bus Driver was a woman I met 2 years ago at a private party. We remembered each other right away and felt grateful for our encounter from our heart of hearts. We admitted to having thought about each other from time to time. We said farewell at my stop, and each of us went on about our business. "As they say, life goes on." "What surprised me and made me extremely happy is that within 2 weeks, she called and invited me to dinner. This came at an appropriate time because I was feeling desperately alone and stressed out in one of my mood swings. Other Drivers always show genuine happiness when I enter the bus. They always ask about my welfare.

Another interesting phenomenon is that some of the female Drivers are so eye- catching, they could be print models for magazine ads. There is a Driver on a major route, who is tall, young and attractive. I cannot make any assumptions of why she is driving a bus for public transportation except that she loves her job. Another gratification of traveling by bus are accommodations for disabled riders. Motorized wheel chair travelers are numerous and assisted with a loading ramp. Once on the bus, the two front three passenger seats, can be pushed up and locked under the windows. This makes space for the wheel chair. Folks in hover rounds, as they are called, ride the bus day and night. I admire the challenges they face on a daily basis. To be quite honest, I decided not to replace my car, after losing it over a year ago. Walking has become a life saving exercise. Especially, since the attitude of all the Bus Drivers keep a smile on my face. In addition, during the rainy season, I can call a cab.

Sandra, looks down at Hope. "Well, baby what do you think?" "Is it readable?" Hope stands up and cocks her head. Sandra lights another cigarette. "Yeah, this will do." She takes a puff coughs up phylum and keeps on puffing. Hope looks at her and whines in desperation her eyes blinking with fear. Sandra picks up Hope and puts her on her lap. "I know baby, you're saying Mommy don't kill yourself." "Don't worry I won't. At least I don't think so." Sandra moves to her Lazy Boy chair and sits down with Hope in her arms. They both fall asleep.

Sandra dreams about being in the Court House in front of the Judge who had sentenced her to 5 years without a Driver's License and 6 weeks of rehabilitation at the Passage Center in North Florida. The Court paid the fees for her detoxification. Her mind wandered to the Spanish designed layout of the Center. The Welcome Hacienda sits behind a circular drive. Sandra gets out of the Court ordered car, and walks to the entrance. Inside, she looks around at the beautifully appointed walls and curtain covered windows. She had heard that this was the "rehab" place for the rich and famous but never expected anything like this. After registration at the oak wood desk, she was escorted to her empty, semi-private room.

Her Counselor, Cassie, comes in introduces herself and fills Sandra in on her class schedule, curfews, and sessions with other clients. Cassie told her that she would attend one-hour program classes in the morning, at lunch and in the evening. Sandra reminisces about feeling like a prisoner. Certainly, not her way of living. Cassie goes on, encouraging Sandra to keep a journal. Not so much about her past but what she envisions as her future. Because of fear of her surroundings, Sandra copped an attitude. "I didn't come here on my own. I'm not an alcoholic or a drug addict." I know how to control myself." Cassie says she understands how Sandra feels. "Before you know it, you will be a new and different woman." Cassie goes on. "You'll even stop smoking cigarettes." "That will be the day," Sandra moans. "I have to have some addiction. Sandra bellows. "No, you do not. Just put your mind to it and all things will come true. Do not forget you also have COPD to keep under control. You do want to live don't you?" "I don't know," Sandra responses. Cassie says, "There's an old Chinese proverb, I want you to remember; *It is time not to be afraid of growing slowly, but afraid of only standing still."*

She remembers her roommate coming into the room after a meeting. The petite, blond with a curvy body was jubilant with enthusiasm. "Hi, my name is Amy," she says as she holds out her hand to Sandra. They shake hands. Amy goes on, "I just came from a hell of a meeting." "What about?" "The reason we're here, silly. About recovery," Amy blurts. "Right." Sandra sighs. "No, listen it was about what recovery is. There are two parts. Abstaining and taking a new approach to life. This includes new ways of thinking and acting that can help us enjoy healthy, loving relationships, good health and personal growth." Sandra's eyes widen as she struggles to wake up.

She immediately picks up her cell phone and calls one of her favorite dealers. "Pedro, come on over here with you know what. It is time to party." While she waits for Pedro, Sandra snorts the last of her cocaine and drinks a glass of wine. She picks up a picture from a side table of her and Joey in his high school band uniform. She kisses the frame and dials Joey's number. There is no answer."Hey honey, it's Mom. Call me back when you get this message. I still have the same number." She looks at the ceiling, wailing, "please stop treating me like this, you're MY GOD. Help me." Sandra sips on her wine. She dials Pedro's number. No answer. She leaves a message. "Pedro, don't come over here. I've changed my mind."

She decides to take Hope out for a walk. In the mid afternoon sun,

Sandra walks Hope to the neighbor hood Park. She sits on a bench with her elbows on her knees and holds Hope's leash while watching kids swing. She speaks aloud. "Oh, Joey how I wish I could meet my new grand daughter," she straightens up pulls Hope's leash and leaves the Park. When she gets home, Pedro, a handsome Latino in his 30's, is standing at her front door. "I was so happy to hear your voice I couldn't wait to see you," he says slapping Sandra's backside. "I left you a message not to come over." "Didn't get that one," he says with a sly smile. She looks around unlocks the door and motions for Pedro to come in.

Once inside, Pedro reaches in his pocket and hands her a small plastic bag of rock cocaine and a bag of marijuana. "You can keep the Pot. Every time I smoke it, my throat feels raw." "That's why I don't smoke it anymore," he says. "Can you give me a couple of days to pay you? I have to pay my rent and utility bill." "I'm running a little short myself. "Do not worry you know I will pay you. I always do." "Okay. But, I can't make this another habit," Pedro echoes. "I found some more jewelry that I can pawn. I'll pay you tomorrow night". "Are there any other special favors I might get for doing this good deed after I get paid?" "How about right now?" Sandra winks.

She leads Pedro into the bedroom. They lay down on the bed, Pedro unbuttons her shirt, and kisses her nipples, taking her back to the eroticism she had with Monique and Eugene. Pedro takes off his clothes and throws them on the floor. Lying beside her, he implores her to, "touch it, kiss it," pointing to his penis. Sandra does as she is told, bringing loud groans from Pedro. That is it baby. You got me going now. Don't stop." "What about me," Sandra yelps. This ain't no freebie." "I got something for you. "Give it to me now." She stops kissing and starts caressing him. " Get it out of my pants pocket. It's all for you." She takes two small packs of cocaine out of his pant pocket, and puts them under her pillow. "Okay, you got it boyfriend."

Sandra does as she is told and brings Pedro to an earth shattering groaning, laughing, climax. He bounces back against the pillow, shaking his body back and forth. "Whoa, Lady you sure know how to please this boy." "Never said I couldn't". I hope this isn't the last time? He wonders. "With you, it probably won't be the last time. But I don't do this with every one and I don't want you to think I'm just some whore looking for hits." "Not you, sister, I respect you," Pedro says. He looks at the bedroom window. "What are those big brown spots," he asks. "Baby frogs," they're all around the building and so are baby lizards, Sandra laughs as she gets out of bed. "They're the real frogs, she says as she scratches her vagina. "And the Cat Lady lives next door." "What do you mean?" "My neighbor feeds 7 or 8 feral cats every day." So you'll always see them close by." "I noticed them I thought they were strays," Pedro muses.

"Okay, up and at em, Man" I have to work on my newspaper column" Pedro gets up and dresses. Sandra goes to her laptop. Her mind is a blank. Hope stares up at her, with shiny eyes and pouty face. She lets out a breath as the phone rings. At the same time, Pedro walks out of the bedroom. She waves him out the door as she answers the phone.

Hi, Spencer she giggles. How is the toothless wonder doing? Sure, I will go to dinner with you. What time will you pick me up? "What? You don't have a car. Neither do I. You want me to take a bus, she says in disbelief. The *Gigolo* restaurant is too far on a bus. Besides, isn't that a fancy restaurant on your income? Okay pick me up in a taxi. My address is 20 Orchid Lane, in Tequesta." Sandra changes her clothes and puts on a long black dress with a crystal elephant brooch. She sprays her hair, puts on make-up and perfume. She picks up Hope hugs her and walks out the door.

While waiting outside on her porch, she thinks about her stash. Ohhhhh. I can always do a hit while I am waiting, she laughs. She rushes back into her apartment. Grabs a rock from the pack under the pillow and takes a hit. Outside she hears a horn blowing. At the same time, the phone rings. She answers it. Hey, Monique, I am going out to dinner with Spencer Madison, you know the guy I met at the hospital. We're going to *Gigolo's*. I'll call you when I get home." She hangs up the phone and yells out the door. "Okay, I'm coming."

Spencer is standing outside holding the car door open. He looks a bit sloppy to Sandra's elegant look. He is wearing loose fitting jeans and a wrinkled shirt. Sandra could not help but say. "You look like you're going to a barbeque, not a fancy restaurant," she says in disbelief. Spencer shrugs his shoulders. "Can't make everybody happy." They get in the cab and ride off.

At the entrance to the restaurant the Maitre,'d tells Spencer that all gentleman diners wear a tie. "We can assist you," he goes on. He reaches behind his desk and hands Spencer a tie. "You can put it on in the Men's Room around the corner." Spencer takes the tie and goes on his way. "I know what you are thinking, Jeffrey, Sandra blurts out. He is a friend I met at the hospital. "If you don't mind my saying Ms. Walker, I know you have and can do better than that." "I know but maybe he can change" "Not at his age. He's been like that too long." "You'll probably right." "Here he comes." "Thank you sir." Jeffrey says to Spencer. Please follow me to your table." Jeffrey seats them at a table in the back. Sandra understands and shakes her head with a pout. Even though they are an inter-racial couple, she was treated much better when she was at the restaurant with Eugene. She reaches over and straightens the tie for Spencer.

Once seated, a Waiter comes to the table to take a drink order. "I'll have a martini." Sandra orders quickly. Spencer orders a diet soda. "You don't drink?" "Not anymore. I've been sober for 10 years." "Then what are you doing with me?" "I like you. When I first laid eyes on you at the hospital, I knew you were the one for me. He opens a small velvet box takes out a small, diamond, engagement ring. "Will you marry me," he asks. "No, I just met you. I don' know where you live or who you really are."

"I've lived in an Assistant Living facility for the last 2 years." The Waiter brings the drinks. Sandra orders another. Then she proposes a toast. She lifts her glass. Spencer is confused. "Come on Sandra implores, let's toast." "I don't know what you mean, I've never done that before." "What? Okay she says patiently. We lift our glasses with the right hand, give the reason for the toast, like to happiness for Sandra and Spencer and then we click the glasses together." She follows through with her lesson by taking a sip from her glass. "Come on take a sip." Spencer sips his soda and smiles. "Do you have children?" she asks. "Never been married have no kids," he replies.

After leaving the restaurant, Spencer has the taxi drop Sandra off at her apartment. He escorts her to the door, kisses her on the cheek and says good night. As soon as she opens the door, Hope happily barks and runs around her with her tail wagging. Sandra instantly, goes to her stash and prepares a hit of crack. After smoking the two packs she got from Pedro, she starts coughing. "Damn it I should have kept the Pot.

This will keep me up all night long." She picks up Hope and sits down on the Lazy Boy chair. She tries to sleep, but remains restless.

"Might as well start writing another column. Not now, Sandra." she says aloud. "Let's go to bed and really get some rest." She starts coughing, wheezing and losing her breath. She cannot stop. "Come on girl, get yourself together." There is a knock on the door. Sandra opens it to discover Monique dressed in a revealing, form fitting, mini dress. "I thought you might be home by now. I can't believe what I heard". "What are you talking about?" Sandra wheezes. "Your new boyfriend works at the *Mandarin* strip bar." "Doing what?," "Come on let's go find out," Monique winks.

Once inside the *Mandarin* Sandra and Monique walk to the bar. There is a male staff of muscle bound young men. Most of the clientele are women. A clock chimes 12 times. An Announcer's voice resonant over slow, guitar music. On stage, are three large gold poles from ceiling to floor. On the opposite sides of the center pole, two scantily clad female strippers slide down the poles and begin taking off their costumes. The Announcer goes on, "Ladies and Gentlemen for your pleasure, please welcome, "Mighty Ram." A well-developed male stripper slides down the center pole. He is dressed in tight red white and blue Speedo shorts, knee high white socks and a red mask He dances around the pole to the music while the stripper's plaster erotic caresses on him from head to toe. The crowd jumps out of their seats and goes wild.

Sandra says to Monique, "that looks like Spencer." "Don't you see, it is?" Monique laughs. "I didn't know he had such six-pack abs." "Neither did I." You mean you haven't slept with him yet,?" Monique says in surprise. "No." "I bet he can make you fly, girl." "No doubt. When the show is over, "Mighty Ram" gets a standing ovation and patrons begin chanting his name. "Mighty Ram, Mighty Ram, Mighty Ram…."

The lights dim and Sandra orders a Rum and Coke and lights a cigarette. Monique orders a beer. "How'd you find out about his job?" Sandra asks Monique. "One of the models I work with comes here all the time." "I wonder why he doesn't get his teeth fixed?" "Must be part of his character. Besides, he never smiled. Just a come hither grin." "Yeah, he probably feels that the best part of him is his body. I've never seen such sexy legs on a man." Sandra says. "He's hot." "Should we let him know we're here?" Monique asks. "Why not?" "I've never felt like this before. It's quite a surprise," Sandra says dreamily. "I think I'm falling in love." "Oh, come on, you can't be serious." "Well, you've got to admit that he's different. Besides that, he's kind, caring and understanding. And those legs are to die for." Sandra goes on. "If the spirit moves you, go for it." Monique inputs. "I already have." Sandra says laughing.

Spencer makes his way to the bar through a group of appreciative female guests who grab his arms. He walks up to Sandra and stares at her with his piercing baby blue eyes. So what are you doing here my sweet?" "Watching you drive women crazy." Sandra says as she eagerly hugs him. "My imagination is running away with me." She calls to the Waiter, "drinks all around." ","Not me Spencer," claims. "I'll have my usual diet soda." The Waiter nods and smiles. "How can you work in a place like this and not drink?" Monique asks. "Just don't need to." "Boy, you have real control. Have you heard that old saying that you can't hang around a barber shop to long without getting a haircut?" Monique goes on. "Sure have." "It fits you perfectly,"

Sandra adds lighting another cigarette. Spencer, jerks the cigarette out of Sandra's mouth. "Look lady, I didn't give you the ring so you could die on me get some sense into your head, stop smoking." Monique claps her hands and shouts "yes." "Okay you two I get the message. I'll do my best." Sandra promises. The waiter delivers the drinks. Spencer tells him they are on his tab. Sandra begins wheezing, says she does not feel well and passes out.

Sandra wakes up in a room at the Persona Nursing Home. Oxygen hose is in her nose and IV is in her right arm. Spencer and Monique are by her side. Spencer is holding her hand, "its time for you to have a change of scenery" he says scruffily. "With all your ailments I think you should go see your son and his family. Therefore, I am buying you a round trip ticket to New York. In the meantime, we are going to work on your recovery. As you well know, it's a lifelong process." "Joey doesn't want to see me," she proclaims. "He won't even talk to me and I can't understand why."

"Write him a letter, let him know you're working on changing your values. And that you're making needed life changes," Spencer insists. "Okay, I'll write to Dina, maybe she'll read it. It is time for me too take out an insurance policy. Especially one with a burial provision. I'll ask for my granddaughter's full legal name and date of birth." "You mean you don't know that information?" Monique says shocked. "Remember, I told you, we've hardly talked over the last couple of years."

"Don't make the letter sound like you dying to see them." Monique insists. "Just let them know that its time to make up for the wrongs." "Yeah," Spencer adds, "you're balancing out your life." Let them know you're getting married." "Not any time soon," Sandra shoots back."When I die, I want to be cremated here in Florida. The proper policy will cover the expenses. I'll start checking online for the best offers from different insurance companies."

"And if you won't marry me, let us at least live together. If it is all right with you, I would like to give up my room at the assisted living facility and move in with you. Get well so you can take care of me," Spencer adds. "I have to go into the hospital. The Doctor found cancer in my bladder. I have to have surgery" "Sweetheart, why didn't you tell me before?" Sandra sobs. "I just found out. In any event, I will be in the hospital for a few days. A lot shorter time than you will be. This time they're going to keep you here until your COPD is under control." The nurse comes in with a nebulizer. "Time for your breathing treatment Ms. Walker." Spencer and Monique leave.

Sandra closes her eyes and thinks about her future. She murmurs to her self. "Why can't I experience the joys of living? I need to know what to do," she whines. A Nun comes into the room. "Hello," she says. "Thought you'd like to discuss a little bit about life." Sandra takes the mouthpiece of the nebulizer out of her mouth and turns off the machine. "You're here at the perfect time she says. I'm so stressed, sad and lonely I don't know what to do."

"You're not alone. Never think that way. God is always with you." "I miss him in my life and the way he makes me feel inside. He gives me pride and self-esteem." "More than that he can give you all the love you need." "I can't stop thinking of this man Spencer who's come into my life. We're living together and he's wonderful, but I don't know what to do about him or with him." "The answers to all your fears come in time," the Nun adds. "I'll drop by tomorrow. You're in my prayers," the Nun walks out. Sandra closes her eyes.

Later that evening, Spencer and Chad , an overweight gray hair, good-looking man in his 50's walk into the hospital room carrying a cake and balloons. "How you feeling Sweetheart?" Spencer asks. "Who's your friend?" Sandra retorts. "Hi my name is Chad." "I didn't know you knew such a hot looking man." Sandra teases. "I haven't seen Chad in years. We met by chance the other day at a bus stop. I told him about you. He suggested that he make you this cake." "How nice. I needed something to take away my boredom." "Now that I'm meeting you I wish I had made you some cupcakes too," Chad interjects." Are you a Chef?" "No I just love to cook and bake. For pretty ladies that is."

"Chad is staying at the apartment for a few days to help me recover from my cancer surgery." "How nice of him." "I think so to, especially since they told me you'd be here for two months". "Who told you that? The Doctor told me this morning I should be out of here in a few days. The COPD symptoms are under control. No more wheezing and my body is responding to the medicine. Besides, our apartment is too small, there is no place for Chad to sleep except the sofa." "That's where he's sleeping now". "But, you told me they got all the cancer out of your bladder. And neither one of us needs a nurse." "Well, it's a little late for that. He checked out of the motel. All his clothes are at our apartment." "Don't worry Miss Sandra I'll be gone before you get home," Chad promises. Spencer reassures Sandra, "When I look in your eyes all I see is what our love can really be. Nothing can take my love away from you. Your love is all I need. The three of us can make it work." "With Hope of course." "By the way, how is my baby?" "Just fine, Spencer smiles. "Missing you."

"And you don't have to worry about cooking," Chad offers. "I scrambled a dozen eggs for Spencer this morning." "That's probably why he invited you to stay with us. You will do all the cooking. Then he'll fart day and night." A habit I have a hard time accepting." "That's cause he eats to fast. All gone in 5 minutes," Chad admits. "Never seen a man eat as much or as fast as he does." "Okay, boys. It is time for me to get out of here and get back to being me. Luckily, I have been able to keep up my newspaper column. I told my readers that I was on vacation." But, don't know what to do with the clients at the ad agency they're getting impatient." Sandra wails. "What's Mighty Ram going to do?" Chad asks. "Keep working it helps pay the bills," Spencer responds.

Within a week, Sandra is discharged from the hospital. We see her at the newspaper office talking with the Publisher. "Why do you want me to keep writing about riding the bus for the next few weeks? There is more to life than sitting at bus stops." "Because that is what you, do best the weary, wheel chair bound, Publisher replies. "There is not much else to do. If I had not had the stroke I would not be closing the office," he goes on. "I don't know what I'm going to do without this job," Sandra laments.

Sandra and Spencer are picked up at their apartment by Chad. His car is close to a wreck. It is an old Plymouth. On the passenger side, the window is taped with gray and black masking tape from one side to the other. Wire is holding the back bumper up in three places. Inside, the visors are taped to the front window. The steering wheel is also taped. With all its mangled, toy car trappings the car runs with precision. Chad drives in the slow lane and keeps pumping the brakes. They are taking Spencer to work. Sandra sits in the back seat frowning and shaking her head. "How do I get myself into these predicaments?" she whispers to herself in disgust. She asks Chad to drop her off at the *Hideaway.* " I will find a ride and be home later," she says to Spencer. He blows her a kiss.

At the *Hideaway*, Sandra walks into the crowded room. Country and Western music plays in the background. She sits at a booth and thinks about Peggy. She remembers their happy times playing volleyball at the beach. She lowers her head when a Lionel Ritchie song, *3 Times a Lady*, begins playing. Her bar friend Pippy walks over and gives her a stuffed animal from the "Treasure Chest." vending machine. He kisses her on the cheek. She returns the kiss and says thank you. "This makes a dozen of these babies you've given me she gushes. What a friend you are." Monique joins her. "Hey lady, what's going on in that head of yours?" I was thinking about Peggy." "I miss her too." She would want us to be happy. Let's go see Spencer perform." "You got a deal," Sandra agrees.

At the *Mandarin*, Spencer is finishing his first show. He sees Sandra and Monique and waves. They wave back as they order their drinks. He joins them at the bar. Monique, quips, "I have an idea. Let's all go to church tomorrow." Spencer, laughs, "I haven't been to church in years." "It could be exciting," Sandra adds. The only excitement I'd have would be to masturbate in front of the congregation," Spencer teases. Sandra responds in an angry voice," How can you be such a dimwit talking about the church like that?" She slaps Spencer. "You're an idiot. Let's go Monique," Sandra fumes. The women abruptly leave.

On Sunday morning, Sandra and Monique sit in a Prayer Circle at church. They hold hands with the other Parishioners and bow their heads in prayer. After their prayers, the women walk out of the sanctuary and down the block. Sandra lights a cigarette. Dressed in his Sunday best, Spencer approaches them. Sandra turns away. He walks in front of her."Give me a chance he pleads. I acted like a fool last night. I'm sorry." Monique smiles. Sandra frowns. "I'm here to attend the service with you," Spencer adds. "Then go inside. I don't want to be around you," Sandra says stonily."Come on Sandra, somewhere in the good book, it has to say forgive and forget." Monique insists. Sandra looks at Spencer, takes a deep breath and holds his hand.

After the church service, the trio enjoys lunch at a nearby restaurant. "I have to start looking for another job," Sandra moans. "Not an easy task," Monique claims. "Sure isn't, the last time I went out on the job circuit all my competition were thirty year olds." "Why don't you take the time off to visit Joey and his family? Remember, I told you I'd pay for the trip." Spencer reminds Sandra."You know I think I'm going to take you up on your offer." Monique and Spencer applauded.

After lunch, Monique drops Sandra and Spencer off at their apartment. "You were very quiet on the way home," Spencer says. "I'm having a mood swing. Not quite sure what I really want to do." "I know what I want to do," Spencer says smoothly. He leads Sandra to the sofa and slowly undresses her. He then takes off his clothes. He pushes Sandra back on the sofa and removes her silk underwear.

While touching her breasts, he smells her panties then puts them on his head and around his face.

At the same time, Sandra pumps his penis up and down.

He pushes her head towards his penis. She locks her mouth around it. Their smooth, intertwined bodies, climax in harmonious copulation. Spencer lies back on the sofa. He licks his upper lip, in pleasure, with his tongue. Sandra is breathless. She takes out an inhalant and takes a puff. They look at each other and smile in satisfaction.

Sandra is in the bedroom packing her luggage for the long awaited trip to New York. She is dressed in pants and a sweater. Her hair is short and parted in the center. Spencer and Chad take her to the airport.

Hope sits on Sandra's lap during the journey. They leave Hope in the car and walk Sandra to the Security Gate. "Have a wonderful time, my darling," Spencer says. Chad kisses her on the cheek. "Take care of my baby," Sandra jokes. "You mean Spencer," Chad asks. "You know who I mean, my baby Hope," Sandra shoots back. "And don't forget to pick up my car after they change the timing chain." "Done deal," Spencer promises.

At the airport in New York, Joey, his wife Dina and their daughter Chloe, meet Sandra at the gate. They hug and kiss each other lovingly. "Mom, I'm so glad to see you. I never thought you'd look this good." "Nor did I." Sandra smiles as she holds Chloe. "It's about time we mend our ways," Sandra offers. Joey drives the car into the driveway of their small house in the woods. "I never thought you would live in such seclusion." "The property and house was given to us four years ago as a wedding gift from Dina's family." Inside the house, the main decorations are miscellaneous items of antique furniture. Dina escorts Sandra to her room.

"Hope this is good enough for you" Dina says with pursed lips. "Why shouldn't it be?" Sandra asks. "Oh, I've heard a lot about your glamorous past life. Both the good and the bad." "Let's get something straight. I did not come here to relive negatives with you or my son. In fact, you're not the person I thought you would be," Sandra says in disappointment. "Why are you really here?" "Listen, Dina, I have and have had a lot of physical problems. It's time to make amends before I go on to meet my Maker." "So, now you're religious, Dina goes on. Joey comes into the room. "What are you two talking about?" "Life," Sandra grins. "Mom, we're having dinner with Dina's family at a restaurant in town. So you might want to freshen up before we go". "You're right son. I'll be with you in a few moments."

Dina walks out of the room with Joey. Sandra closes the door. "I don't like her," Dina pouts. "You don't even know her yet. Give her a chance." "Like she gave you?" "Sure she was hard to live with when I was growing up but she's still my Mother." "Joey, don't you see she's putting up a front to make you think she's changed?" "I don't believe that. Before you turn and walk away from her Dina. Think about how you feel in your heart of hearts." Joey takes her in his arms, they hug and kiss. Chloe walks into the room. "Where's Grandma? I like her I want to see her." "She's in her room getting dressed. She'll be with us in a moment," Joey promises.

At the restaurant, Sandra is introduced to Dina's parents, a few aunts, uncles and cousins. In all, ten people attend the dinner. Sandra looked radiant. Her dazzling smile quickly enveloped the family, especially the men. Dina is surprised and stunned. The least of what she expected. Sandra tells them stories of her life in the fast lane during the good old days. She also compliments Joey about his job as a Manager at a Loan company and Dina's pride in motherhood.

For the duration of her one week visit, Sandra out does herself in pleasing all who cross her path. Finally, Dina drops her guard and accepts her beleaguered ill health Mother-In-Law. The trip takes its toll on Sandra who suffered more and more from COPD symptoms. She carried her inhalants with her and used them discreetly. Joey was extremely proud of his Mother, which left him flabbergasted. Even with her ailments, he never expected her to be so giving, loving and carefree.

The week went by fast for Sandra just as she wanted it to. At the airport in New York, she was bid good-bye at the gate by Joey, Dina and Chloe. Long, tight hugs and kisses were shared. A satisfied Sandra walked through the gate with a special walk swollen with pride. She had accomplished the reason for her venture. The return of the long lost love between her and Joey, her one and only son.

In Florida, Spencer and Chad were waiting at the gate. They immediately noticed Sandra's tired, worn appearance. Spencer takes her in his arms. They walk to Chad's car. "Why didn't you drive my car?" Sandra asks. The timing chain was supposed to be replaced by the time I got home. And you were going to pick it up when the job was finished." "I did. You're not going to like this," Spencer says slowly. "I drove your car to work last week and it was stolen from the parking lot at the *Mandarin* over the weekend." "Stop joking," Sandra laughs.

"I wish I was. I filed a police report. Haven't hear from them yet." "I'm sick of your jokes," Sandra wails. "He's not joking, Miss Sandra," Chad interjects. "Stay out of this, you Bastard." They walk to Chad's car parked at the curb. Sandra starts to wheeze. "I need to go to the drug store," Sandra states. "I ran out of my medication in New York." "No problem," Spencer claims. "Where's Hope?" "At home, she's a bit under the weather. Been sneezing a lot." "Forget the drug store. Take me home I want to see her, now."

Chad pulls his car up to the apartment building. Sandra jumps out. She runs to the door and unlocks it. Hope is nowhere to be found. Sandra looks under the bed and finally finds Hope laying on a towel under the dining room table. Sandra picks her up. Hope licks her face. "Oh, my poor baby. What's wrong? We'll get you to the VET." Hope gives her a pitiful stare. Spencer comes in with the luggage. "I have to go to work early. Need to make more money" "I know. Have a good afternoon." "Don't let anyone rape you," she laughs. "Hasn't happened yet. But, I've been close to it," Spencer jokes.

In the apartment, Sandra pours a glass of wine. She picks up the phone and calls Monique. There is no answer. Sandra leaves a message. "Hi, Monique. Back from New York. Really need to talk to you." Hope walks over and looks up at her. Sandra reaches down and strokes her soft, smooth, coat of fur. Hope sneezes and wags her tail. Sandra calls the VET. "Hi this is Sandra Walker. Need to make an appointment for my dog, Hope. She's sneezing a lot. Okay, I'll bring her in right now." Thunder roars in the background. Sandra walks to the door and looks outside. Dark clouds gather overhead. "Just like my life," she snorts.

The phone rings. "Hey Monique. It was a great trip, except for Dina. She's determined to not like me. I'm not sure why. Maybe, because of my closeness with Joey. In the end she was cordial. But, she couldn't wait for me to leave." And to make matters worse my car was stolen. That's right. Girl, I'm so mad I could kill the Mother Fucker. I'm sick of him. All Spencer was supposed to do was pick up the car from the mechanic, and drive it home" Sandra takes a sip of wine. "No, I didn't drink or do drugs while I was there. I would like to talk to you about a business proposition. Well, I was thinking, there are still two clients on the books at the ad agency. Between the two of us, I think we could make them happy with new and different ad campaigns. I know you are good with sales. You do that all the time with your modeling clients. They're buying your talents to sell their products. Okay, think about it. Talk to you soon". Sandra hangs up the phone, puts Hope in her kennel, walks out the door and hails a passing taxi.

Later, Sandra returns to the apartment. Spencer is asleep in the bedroom. She stands at the foot of the bed and stares at him. His legs are crossed. He is moving the top leg back and forth, thumping it against his foot. She shakes her head back and forth in confusion as she lays down beside him. He wakes up. "Hello, my sweet," he says. "Hi, darling. Sandra puts her arm around his body. "There's something I've wanted to talk to you about for a long time." "What's that?" "Why do you thump your foot against the other when you're in bed?" "I've been doing that since I was eight years old. My Grandfather made me do it when I would lay in front of him watching television." "Why?" "He wanted to make sure I wasn't asleep." "And all these years, you've never stop doing it." "That's right."

"A strange habit," Sandra adds. "Anyway, Hope doesn't have a cold and I got all her shots. She was not to happy with that. But, she's all right. I've been thinking about calling Pedro." "If that's what you want, go ahead." "You have any extra cash?" "Not for that." "Maybe he'll give me credit. I've paid him all I owe." Sandra picks up the phone and dials. "Hey, Pedro. Yes, I'm back. Can you come over. I'll take the usual. Oh, and can you give me credit until I get to the bank? I have money left in my saving account. Great." Sandra hangs up the phone. "Pedro will be over in half an hour." Spencer gives her an unhappy look. "I'm going for a walk," he says. He gets up and leaves the room.

Pedro knocks on the door. As soon as Sandra opens the door he sweeps her in his arms. "Whoa, wait a minute boyfriend. Not here not now. Spencer could be coming back anytime." Pedro shows a look of disappointment as he backs away. He hands her a plastic bag. "Okay," he says. "When will I see you again?" "During the week," she answers. "I'll call you when I know Spencer is doing a double shift,' she winks. Pedro salutes her and walks towards the door as Spencer opens it. He holds the mail and a newspaper in his hand. "How ya doing, Pedro?" Could be better, man," Pedro snorts in frustration.

Sandra sits on the sofa and opens the plastic bag. She takes out a piece of cocaine and puts it on the table. Spencer stares at her for a moment with a sickened look on his face, then goes into the bedroom. Sandra does her hit and lays back on the sofa. She grins and begins to prepare another dose. Spencer walks into the room with a check in his hand. "This came in the mail today. Did you write a check for $400.00 on my account?" "What?" "Come on you can tell me the truth." "I wouldn't do that." "Let me see it." "The date is when I was in the hospital." "You're right. I didn't notice that." "Spencer, have you left your check book laying around?" "Only, on the dresser in the bedroom. Well, I'm not going to worry about it now. I have to catch the bus and get to work." Spencer leaves. Sandra takes her last hit.

Sandra calls Monique. "I think I know who wrote the check. The creep. He's a con artist. We've been good to him letting him stay with us. I don't trust him. It is time you and I talk seriously. Will you pick me up?" Monique and Sandra chat at a table in a small, quiet, café. "The way I see it, is we contact the Duffy Brothers and tell them we can publish the children's adventures book every month for their 500 restaurants. And we'll give a discounted rate during the first 6 months." Sandra suggests.

"That all sounds well, and good but first we need to see if your team is still with you." Monique adds. "Not my team our team. And yes they are. I talked to the Artist the printer and bookkeeper last week. They want Eugene's memory to live on. Ivory Advertising Corporation is not dead." "Have you talked to Spencer?" "For what? He doesn't know anything about advertising or publishing. Besides, I'm having trouble living with him. All he does is sleep all day. And I hate Chad in the apartment especially sleeping on the floor. It's time for a change. I deserve better." "You're the boss," Monique, smiles. Good, let's go to the *Hideaway* and celebrate our new beginnings.

Chad sits at the bar of the *Mandarin*. He takes a shot of liquor and chases it down with a gulp of beer.

Spencer joins him. He holds the check in his hand. "I know you did this," Spencer announces. He throws the check on the bar. "The question is why? You've committed fraud, asshole." "I needed some money, man. I'm gonna pay you back. I just got a job." "What kind of job? I'm working for this guy in Alabama as a Courier." "Doing what?" "He calls me and tells me to pick up money at Western Union. Then I deposit it in a bank account." "Are you crazy?" "No. I get $5.00 for every hundred I deposit." "You're risking your freedom for that?" "It's better than nothing." Spencer shakes his head in revulsion.

"Look I don't play games. I want my money back. If Sandra finds out about this, she'll go crazy. You know she wants you out of the apartment anyway" I promise I'll pay you. Let's not. mention anything to Sandra," Chad pleas. "She already knows." "I'll pay you back and find a place to live." Spencer grabs Chad's collar. "You've got 60 days, Shit head or you'll really be sorry." "I have to get ready for work." "I promise to do what you ask, Chad whispers. Spencer pushes him against the bar and heads to the dressing room. Chad lets out a long breath.

Sandra speaks on the phone in her apartment. Monique sits next to her holding Hope. "Yes, Mr. Duffy, This is Sandra Walker calling from Ivory Advertising in Florida. Have you ever been here? It's beautiful. Thank you for your condolences. Eugene will always have a special part in my heart. We wanted you to know that we can carry on with our production of your fun and activity book. It will still be a four color, newspaper print book, including the 3 main characters, a 6-page adventure story, pen pals, coloring page, letters page and a membership application to the club. We'll also give you a 10% discount on your order of 500 books per case. I understand. Thank you for letting me take your time. Like to hear from you as soon as possible." Sandra hangs up the phone. "He's interested", she tells Monique.

"I'm going to call Joey and Dina. Let them know how much weight I gained from all the good meals they fed me. And talk to Chloe" "Good idea," Monique agrees. "Ummm, or maybe I should call Pedro first." Come to your senses. You've got to stop smoking all that crap," Monique states "I know, I know, but it takes time." "Why don't you go to one of those meetings where they help people with addictions?" Don't start pushing me. I know what I'm doing. I am not an addict. Boy, you sure forget your past fast. Okay Monique this visit is over. I'll call when I need you," Sandra says in anger. Alright, but don't lose the last 3 months. I admire you for quitting cold turkey. And you've been doing really well by getting everybody back on track and ready to work." Monique claims. "And I've done it all by myself." Monique frowns, puts Hope on the floor and leaves.

Sandra takes a puff from an inhaler. She lights a cigarette, picks up the phone and dials. "Hey, Joey it's Mom. I'm doing great. I must have gained 10 pounds during my visit. Some of my clothes are too tight. But, that's okay. I'll get rid of it. My main concern is putting Ivory Advertising back on the map. What happened? You lost your job?" I'm sorry to hear that. The company closed. The same thing happened with me at the newspaper office. If it weren't for Spencer, I don't know how I'd make out. Most of my savings are gone. And my car was stolen. We haven't opened an office yet. I'm working with Monique from home. These days, all you need is an address, a laptop and a cell phone to run a business. I hope you find a job soon. How's Dina and Chloe? Tell them I said hello when they get home. I'll call you next week."

Sandra dials another number. "Hi, Pedro. I know its been a long time. Can you come over tonight about nine o'clock?" Just half of what I usually order. No, I am not joking, Sandra hangs up the phone. Spencer walks in from the bedroom. "I heard that phone call." "Right, it's going to help me lose all this weight I've gained. I don't even feel comfortable naked in front of you." "There are better ways to lose weight." "I know, but they're boring." I just talked to Joey. He lost his job." "That's too bad." "I'd like to offer him a job with me when I can rent an office. In the meantime, I'll send him a check for fifty dollars."

"That's nice of you, and very surprising. Thought all your cash went to your habits," Spencer says. I am still a Mother. At least, I don't go around letting some con artist steal from me and do nothing about it." I want Chad out of here by the end of this week". "I'll be happy to tell him. I'm sick of him too." "What are you going to do about getting your money back?" "He told me that he's going to pay me with money from his new job." "What job?" "He's a Courier for some company in Alabama." "I don't want to hear about it. Just get rid of him." Spencer holds Sandra's hands. "You know I love you. There is nothing I won't do to please you." He takes money out of his wallet and hands Sandra a hundred dollar bill. "Here, take this for your purchase." "I don't know how to thank you. I'm embarrassed," Sandra whispers. Spencer takes her in his arms and kisses her passionately. Spencer suggests that she and Monique join him later at the *Mandarin*. She agrees. He kisses her again and leaves for work.

Sandra calls Monique. "Want to go to the *Mandarin* tonight. Pick me up around 10." There is a knock on the door. Sandra opens it for Pedro. He looks around. "Hey girlfriend, want to come to my house?" "Not a bad idea," Sandra responses. "Come on let's go," Pedro says anxiously.

They walk out to Pedro's car, a late model black with silver trim corvette. He holds the door for Sandra. In the car he hands her an envelope. "Here put this in your purse," he tells her. By the way, I'm giving you your usual order at half the price. That's how much I care about you. Can't stop thinking about our great lovemaking." "Don't you have a girlfriend?" "Not a steady one." They drive into a parking space in front of a duplex with a red door. "Here we are," Pedro announces. He gets out and opens the car door for Sandra.

Inside the apartment, Sandra looks around. One wall is covered with bookshelves filled with an array of titles. There are also paintings and pictures depicting scenes of nature. The small, bedroom apartment is neat and clean. Pedro lights candles on the cocktail table. "Would you like a drink?" "By all means." Sandra says happily. Pedro pours each of them a glass of wine. They sit on the sofa. It starts pouring rain. "We got here just in time," Sandra muses. "Yes, and I love making love when it rains," Pedro whispers in her ear. "Well you better hurry up because you know these Florida rain storms only last for about 5 minutes." Sandra jokes. "You're right about that," Pedro says. Pedro stands up. "Let's go to the bedroom."

Pedro leads her into his candlelit bedroom. Classical music is playing. They sit on the side of the bed. Let me take a hit first, Sandra says as she takes the envelope from her purse. She pulls out her stem and lays a rock of cocaine on top of it as Pedro takes off his clothes. She takes a puff lays the stem on the side table and lays back on the bed. Pedro unbuttons her shirt, and kisses her nipples, Lying beside her, he implores her to, "touch it, kiss it," pointing to his penis. Sandra does as she is told, bringing loud groans from Pedro. "That's it baby."

You got me going now. Don't stop." Sandra continues on and brings Pedro to a devastating, moaning, smiling, climax. He bounces back against the pillow, shaking his body back and forth. "Whoa, Sandra you're the best woman I've ever had." "Was it better than the last time"? "Sure was." Sandra takes a puff from the stem. She looks at her watch. "Hate, to be in a hurry, but I've got to get back home." "My pleasure," Pedro smiles. His phone rings, he answers it. Hey, man been waiting to hear from you. I'll be over in half an hour." Sandra takes another hit while Pedro dresses. "I've got to get back to work, it's a busy weekend, Pedro announces. So let's go." Sandra whispers in his ear.

In her apartment, Sandra takes a shower, and walks into the living room with a towel wrapped around her body. Chad is laying on the sofa. "How you doing Miss Sandra? he asks. "Fine," Sandra says as she turns around walks to the bedroom and slams the door shut. She gets dressed, uses her inhaler then takes a hit from her stem. "What the hell?" she says to her self. She takes out a pill bottle and swallows two pills. She lights a cigarette. There is a knock on the door. "I'm coming Sandra yells." She rushes pass Chad stokes Hope back and opens the door. Monique is waiting. I am ready, I want to get out of here. "Have a good time, Miss Sandra," Chad howls from the sofa.

In the car, Sandra explains her anger to Monique. I told Spencer that idiot had to be out of the apartment by this weekend. And I get home he's laying on the sofa. Where were you?" "Visiting Pedro. He has a cute apartment." "What's wrong with you? We have to tend to a growing business and you're still chasing your stupid highs." "Don't, worry I can handle it." "Doesn't look like it. You're high right now. I have to tell you the truth, if you don't get this curse under control, I am out of the picture." "I understand", Monique. "Spencer and Chad are driving me crazy. Without you I'd be lost. I've already decided that I'm going to find a meeting place to get help." "Now, you're talking. But, promise me you'll follow through," Monique says sternly. "I'll do my best," Sandra sighs.

Monique pulls her car into the parking lot of the *Mandarin.* Sandra and Monique walk to a table. A member of the female staff takes their drink order. Sandra orders a rum and coke, Monique orders a beer. Once again, most of the clientele are women. A clock chimes 9 times. An Announcer's voice reverberates over upbeat, guitar music. On stage, are the three large gold poles from ceiling to floor. On the opposite sides of the center pole, two scantily clad female strippers slide down the poles and begin taking off their costumes.

The Announcer goes on, "Ladies and Gentlemen for your pleasure, please welcome, "Mighty Ram. Spencer slowly slides down the center pole. He is dressed in his usual costume, tight red white and blue Speedo shorts, knee high white socks and a red mask. He circles around the pole to the music while the stripper's plaster erotic caresses on him from head to toe. The crowd applauds. Spencer continues moving with a smug look on his face. Then he starts dancing around the tables closest to the stage. Women reach out and touch his chest and legs.

"I've never seen a man with such sexy legs," Sandra shouts. "The rest of him ain't to bad either." "That's the truth," Sandra echoes. The music stops. Spencer goes back to the stage and bows. The crowd gives him a standing ovation. Instead of joining in on the ovation, Sandra orders another drink. "I don't know what to do with that man. In real life he's a sloppy dresser, has no teeth and has sickening nervous habits." "Why don't you try to help him change?" "He's had some of his problems for years. Like thumping his feet in bed so hard that the bed shakes. And his right hand shakes sometimes. What I can't stand is his constant farting." "Hasn't he seen a Doctor for all this?" "No. And he refuses to do so. He has a list of excuses. Then when he got out of hospital, he told me he has Bi-Polar disorder. Then he changed his mind and said he's Uni-Polar The part I hate the most is that he is always teasing me. And the other dilemma with our relationship is that almost every statement I make to him about anything in the reality of life. He tells me it's not so." "Like what?" "It could be anything I've heard on the news, or something I've read. He constantly tells me I am wrong, makes me feel like a child. He has no class or style."

Spencer joins them. "Did you enjoy the show?" "Of course we did. That's why we're here, to see Mighty Ram drive women crazy," Sandra says. "My performance was all for you, my darling. Are you going to stay for my next show?" "Sure. But, I have to talk to you about Chad. Has he paid you your money?" "He said he would pay me by the end of the week. And you believe him? What else can I do? He's really working for those people in Alabama." "Yeah, and right now, he's laying on the sofa in our apartment." "He can't do anything until they call," Spencer shares. "I'm going to the Ladies Room, order me another drink." Sandra leaves the table as upbeat music begins playing. In a stall in the Ladies Room Sandra sits on the toilet seat fixes her self a hit and puffs. She lets out a long breath, collects her self and grins.

Monique and Spencer wait for Sandra. "I am worried about Sandra, she's still doing drugs and alcohol. She promised me she would stop and she promised to start going to meetings." "We have to leave that up to her. She's a grown woman." "Then why do you treat her like a child sometimes?" "I don't know. I guess because my last girlfriend didn't have the beauty or brains Sandra has. I was in that relationship for 10 years. My girlfriend then was a user and I had to tell her everything to do." "Maybe you two aren't meant for each other," Monique ponders. "We're coming up on our second year together. I truly love her. Like the old saying goes, I'd take a bullet for her." "I don't think she understands your kind of love." "I don't understand it myself."

Sandra returns to the table with a wide smile on her face. Monique and Spencer look at each other knowingly. "Hey, gang," Sandra yelps in a quivering voice. "How about another drink?" "Don't you think you've had enough?" Monique asks. "What?" "Two drinks give me a break." Sandra motions to the waitress as she lights a cigarette. "Give us another round and give Spencer his usual." "So did you two have fun talking about me?" Who said we were doing that?" Monique asks. "Oh I can feel your energy and I saw the knowing look between you." "Okay, Sandra there's no need to lie. We both love you and will stick by your side when you want help."

"If I decide to get help. Monique I thought about what we talked about and it's just to much to quit everything at once and try to run a business." Yes, I know. But, it is to your best interest, especially since you have COPD," Monique counters. With his legs bumping against each other at his knees, Spencer chimes in I'm going to let you ladies carry on. I have to rest before my next show. I'll be in my dressing room if you want to visit."

You see how he was bumping his knees together? That's another nervous habit. He does that all the time." Sandra takes a pill from her purse, swallows it and takes a sip of her drink. "What's wrong with you? "One week of sobriety in New York, and look at you now. Your life is full of one relapse after another." Sandra frowns. "You sure know how to ruin a good high. I am ready to go. You can drop me off at the *Hideaway*. I'm going to meet Thomas there." "You didn't tell me he was in town." "Arrived this morning." "Don't you want me to go with you?" Monique says in disappointment. "Only if you keep your mouth shut. I want him to invest in the ad agency."

Monique parks her car near the *Hideaway*. The parking lot is full. Sandra freshens her make-up and hair. "Nick sure has a lot of business tonight," Sandra notices. They walk into the bar, patrons are sitting at the bar and standing wall to wall. Thomas is sitting at the last available booth, and motions them over. Sandra pushes her way through the crowd saying hello to a few of her bar friends, Monique follows. Sandra rushes up to Thomas and gives him a long hug and kiss." You must be Monique?" "Yes. Nice to meet you." You look fabulous, Sandra. "Must be from seeing Joey last month." "And for me to see you now," "Thank you my dear. How is Joey?" I just found out that he lost his job." "What is he going to do?" He doesn't know yet, They live in a small town, Not much work." Sandra says. "Dina's family is helping them pay the bills."

A waitress comes to the booth and takes their drink orders. Beer for Monique, wine for Sandra and a vodka ice for Thomas. "How long will you be in town" Sandra asks Thomas. "This time around, 2 weeks." "I wanted to talk to you about helping me keeping the agency open." "Have you talked to Jonathon?" "No. All his money is tied up in his boutique. Let me explain what we've done so far, we talked to the Artist, Printer and Accountant. They're ready to keep Eugene's memory alive by working with us." Who is us?" Thomas asks. "Me and Monique and hopefully you.

We talked to the President of Duffy Brothers in Connecticut. Ivory Advertising published their children's activity book for 20 years. They were one of Eugene's first clients. Here's the deal we offered. It will still be a four color, newspaper print book, including the 3 main characters, a 6 page adventure story, pen pals, coloring page, letters page and a membership application to the club. We'll also give them a 10% discount on their order of 500 books per case." "The answer?" "Mr. Duffy is thinking about it."

"Your deal sounds good except for one flaw." "What is that? "There is no need to offer them a 10% discount, especially since they don't know if their product will be the same. I would suggest you print a sample copy to show them what the new look will be like. If they accept it, give them the 10% for the first 6 months. You should also have a website designed for club members, so they can chat online." "That's a wonderful idea, "Sandra gushes.

"Have you thought of the club member ages?" "Yes, the same as before, elementary through junior high school." "Keep in mind, that the book is free to children who eat at the restaurants with their families. I think the age range should be 11 to 15. They would be more interested in reading the stories, participating in the activities in the book, and chatting online." Upgrade the publication to this century."

Thomas looks at Monique, "Now, what's your name again"? "Monique" "Yes", "How do you fit into this picture?" "I am a model who works with an agency. I call prospective clients on the phone for print jobs. I market our services by explaining that we have top rated Photographers, Make-Up Artist and Stylists. If they need a Model of color, I do the job. Our customers include magazines and newspapers. On the roster are 10 permanent regulars. We serve a few of them on a monthly basis." "What's your pay scale?" I work on commission for marketing and sales. When I do modeling jobs it's a flat rate, including expenses. I want to get involved so, I can help Sandra get more clients. She's my best friend so even if it's on a part-time basis, I am willing to do whatever I can to help."

"Has Sandra told you about me?" "Not really. I know you were Eugene's best friend." "I live and work in Vancouver, British Columbia. I come to Florida to enjoy the tropical weather and when I get bored at home. I am not married and don't choose to be. I own a successful insurance agency with a six member staff. He turns to Sandra, oh dear I almost forgot. "How's Hope?" "She's wonderful and as cute as ever. Thank you for asking." "Miss Sandra, you have a great deal of work to do in order to succeed. Are you still drinking and doing drugs?" "Yes, once in a while. Not as much as I've done in the past."

"To be honest with you, I have to tell you that I have COPD." "What's that? "It's an incurable infection, Chronic Obstructive Lung Disease. Cigarette smokers are the prime target. The symptoms include chronic bronchitis and emphysema. COPD makes breathing difficult. I have inhalers that I use and I'm trying to quit smoking." "Did the Doctor tell you how long you will live with this disease?" "He said I could add a few years if I stop smoking. But, I've since met people who've had it for 10-15 years and still keep smoking. My neighbor has it and we're always knocking on each others door buying two or four cigarettes from each other." Do you have a life insurance policy?" Thomas asks. "No, I hoped you would help me." "I will." "I also have been having trouble with my lower back. Serious pain when I sit to long in front of the computer. Have an appointment with a pain management Doctor next week."

"What exactly do you want me to do with your business?" "Invest in the company, we need start-up capital so we can move into an office and not work at my kitchen table." "Have you written a Proposal?" "No." "Then write one about what you want and submit it to me. I'll make a decision after I read it." "But, you're only going to be here for 2 weeks." "I can stay longer if I have to. Shouldn't take that long to write it. You have it all in your head. Except for one ration you didn't mention, what percentage of the business your investors will receive." "That's a difficult one for me. I don't know what to offer." "Talk to your Accountant, he can help you."

Sandra excuses her self and goes to the Ladies Room. She locks the stall door, takes out her stem a piece of cocaine and smokes it. She starts to cough and wheeze. There is a knock at the door. "This stall is taken she wheezes."" I know it is. It's me, Monique open the door." Sandra unlocks the door and practically falls into Monique's arms. "Are you crazy. Thomas is ready to leave. He asked me to come and get you." "Go tell him I'm okay." "I'll be out in a minute." "Are you sure you're okay?" "Yes. Order me a ginger ale." Monique leaves with a disenchanted look on her face. Sandra takes a pill bottle out of her purse, shakes out a pill and takes it by filling her hands with water from the faucet at the bathroom sink. She stands tall, puts on lipstick, smoothes her hair with her hands and walks back to the booth.

"Thomas, why are you leaving us so soon?" "I have an early meeting in the morning." He hands both Sandra and Monique his card. "Call me on my cell phone when the Proposal is ready. Also, call me tomorrow Sandra about the life insurance policy. Both of you are in my prayers." Thomas hugs Sandra and shakes Monique's hand. They sit down at the booth. A waitress comes over, "Angelo wants to buy you ladies a drink." "That's nice," Monique says. "I certainly need one." Sandra orders a shot of rum with a beer back, Monique orders a beer. Sandra makes her way to the jukebox and plays a few of her Motown favorites.

When she returns to the booth, Angelo is sitting next to Monique. "Hi, Angelo. Thanks for the drinks, but if you don't mind I need to discuss serious business with my friend." Angelo gets up bows and leaves. "He seems like a nice man," Monique murmurs."He was hot for Peggy." "And probably any good looking woman with class." "He's not my type at all." What did you think of Thomas? If you can get him to believe that we can make the business work, go for it." I'll call the Accountant in the morning and see what he says." "Right now I feel like I should go home and rest. Are you ready to leave?" When I finish my beer. Sandra takes out her cell phone. "I'm going to call Joey." "With all the noise in here he won't hear you." I'll step outside. Sandra walks to the door and goes outside.

She dials Joey's number and gets the answering machine. "Hi family, it's Mom. Calling to see how all is going with you. Still trying to lose weight from the delicious meals you fed me. Please call me back as soon as you get this message. Need to talk to you about my life insurance policy that I'm subscribing to. Love you." Monique joins Sandra. "Did you talk to him?" "No, had to leave a message. Sandra I think we should go to my place and talk about our future together." "I understand, Monique it is time to stop acting insane." They walk to Monique's car and get in.

They drive up to Monique's small house on a busy street near the beach. "There's a full moon tonight. Let's go sit on the beach," Monique suggests. Monique parks her car in the driveway. "Let's walk, it's only a few blocks." "I know Monique." "You haven't been here so long I thought you might have forgotten." As they walk to the beach Sandra apologizes to Monique for her behavior. "I didn't know what to think of you. I felt like I was accompanying a binger who wanted to overdose." Monique says half-heartily, "You're right. I guess I am at a deadlock over what do to with Spencer. Part of me loves him and the other part says to move away from him." "He can't be that hard to live with." "Yes he is. He teases me all the time. In addition, the money situation is miserable. By the middle of every month, he has no money. He has so many over drawn credit cards that they're all threatening legal action." Doesn't he get a good paycheck from the *Mandarin*?"

"He only gets paid a couple of hundred a week, plus tips. We made a deal when he moved in. He would pay the rent and I would pay everything else, including food, cable TV, the laundry and utilities. My money comes from my Widow's Benefits from Eugene. And when I ask him to do something like take out the garbage, it could take him 3 days and me asking him 4 or 5 times before he does it." His nervous habits are unbearable. In bed, he thumps his feet, making the bed shake and his right hand shakes once in awhile.

Sandra lights a cigarette and starts choking and coughing. "Put out the cigarette," Monique demands. They walk to a bench on the beach and sit down. Sandra gets rid of the cigarette. The sky is filled with stars, the moon is full and bright. Sandra continues on, "and he has no class or style. He always wears sloppy jeans and wrinkled shirts. Even his underwear is droopy. The neatest I ever see him is on stage at the *Mandarin*. At home, he's a slob, leaving unopened mail and magazines wherever he sits. His name should be OHIO (Only Handle It Once). When we watch television together, every time I turn the channel he says he's all ready seen the episode of the series we're watching. Then when I turn on a popular series, he tells me what's going to happen at the end of the show. He even counts my cigarettes to see how many I've smoked in a day. I tell you Monique I can't stand it anymore." Neither can Hope. He's spoiling her to death. There are at least 5 saucers with food laying around the apartment and he feeds her out of his hand with hamburger or bacon he cooks for her. So, now she won't eat unless he feeds her.

"I've had older men in my life in all my marriages. Now, I know why. There was a spiritual side to our relationships. I think of Eugene every day, he was the finest man in my heart of hearts." "Let's concentrate on Spencer's good side." "That's the surprising part that keeps me with him. Besides, the engagement ring he bought me 3 other rings with semi-precious stones. He buys me gifts all the time. A beautiful robe when I was in the hospital, perfume that I don't like and other gifts since we've been together."

"That's the material side of your life with him." Monique notes. "We never shout and scream at each other. I'm the one with negative moods and anger. When I get mad at him, my mood sometimes goes on for 2 or 3 days. A lot of that comes from him teasing me. He can't help himself, and he always laughs after the tease. Then right away he says he sorry." "At least they're only verbal teases," Monique laughs. "You're right. He's never hit me or harmed me physically." "Sounds to me you should both go to a shrink." "He refuses. Do you think by him being Bi-Polar has anything to do with it?" "I don't know ask his Doctor. His Doctor is the person who told him about OHIO" "Sounds like Spencer has no common sense," Monique laughs.

"Well, that's enough about Spencer, somehow I'll be guided in the right direction. I read Tarot cards and my astrology every day. A change is going to come. You believe in that crap?" "Yes, I do." What about GOD?" I know there's a GOD, I have to get to know him better." I know he better have Chad out of the apartment by the end of this week, or I will be the one out. I'm sick and tired of living in the dark in the bedroom." "Give the man a chance. I think he's doing the best he can," Monique says defensibly. "And turn on the light or open the hurricane shutters in the bedroom."

"How old do you think Thomas is?" Sandra asks. "Late 60's. Why"? "Because I'd like to get to know him better. Have him teach me more about the business side of his life." "I have a feeling you want more than that. Don't forget he lives in Canada." "And Florida," Sandra shares. "The last time he was here he bought a condo on the intracostal waterway in Boca Raton." "Let's walk back to my house and talk about the Proposal he wants," Monique suggests. They hold hands and start walking the short distance to Monique's home. "You know, I'll never forget the night I shared with you and Eugene," Monique says. "Had never done that before and haven't since," "Nor have I," Sandra says with sentiment.

They walk to Monique front door, she unlocks it and motions Sandra to go inside. In the living room, dozens of plush animals are on the sofa, chairs and tables. On the walls are pictures of Monique from different photo sessions. Sitting on an antique desk in a corner of the living room is a laptop, printer and scanner. A bulletin board with notes and a large calendar hang on the wall over the desk."Again, welcome to my humble abode. "Thanks, the last time I was here I was too high to enjoy your peace and comfort," Sandra says with an embarrassed look on her face. She takes out her inhaler and takes a puff.

"Have you ever written a Proposal for a business?" Monique asks Sandra. "No, but I saved business plans that Eugene wrote." "Great. They will be our map." "Boy, my body is tired and worn," Sandra wails. There are no drugs here," Monique says. "I wasn't thinking of that," Sandra answers. "I have something for you." Monique walks into her bedroom and returns with a Bible. "This is what I want you to start reading and believing. We should also go to Wednesday night Prayer Service and Sunday Service at my church." "I can't promise all that, but I'll do my best."

"What I want to do is go to meetings and hear other people's stories and share my own." "That's good too. Let's look on the computer and see if we can find a church meeting close to where you live." "Okay." Monique sits down in front of the laptop and turns it on. "While you're downloading, I'm going to the bathroom." Sandra takes her purse and goes to the bathroom. She shuts the door. Inside, Sandra takes out her stem and the last piece of cocaine. Puts it on the stem lights it and puffs. She inhales holds her breath and smiles.

Sandra joins Monique, and sits down besides her. "I found a group that has meetings in downtown Tequesta. They start at seven in the morning 10 in the morning and then one at noon and 6 in the evening. All the meetings last an hour. If you don't like that schedule there's lots of meetings all over the county. Phone numbers are also listed, so you can call for more information. I'll print out the list for you." Monique notices Sandra's paranoid behavior.

"What's wrong?" Thought I heard someone at the door. "I didn't. Relax, calm down. We're on a positive mission here. Don't destroy it," Monique says annoyed. Sandra lights a cigarette. "My shoulders ache, my back hurts and I feel tight and sore", Sandra admits."I'll print out the list then I'll give you a massage." Monique turns on the printer. "Come into the bedroom with me," Monique requests. Sandra follows her.

"Take off your clothes, I'll give you a complete massage". "Great" "Lay on your stomach." Sandra lays down on the bed and lifts her arms over her head. Monique pours lotion on her hands and begins massaging Sandra's shoulders, then her neck and upper back. Monique then goes on to massage Sandra's back, thighs, legs and feet. Sandra falls asleep. Monique pulls a blanket over her and leaves the room with a contented look on her face.

The next morning, Sandra wakes up and sees Monique sleeping in bed beside her. She gently wakes up Monique, "What happened here last night?" "You don't remember? I gave you a massage and you fell asleep." "I better call Spencer, he doesn't know where I am." "He probably came home from work and went right to bed," Monique quips. Sandra dials her cell phone. "Hi sweetie. I spent the night at Monique's. Is Hope okay? I'll be home in a little while." Monique gets up. "I'm going to take a shower. Want to take it with me? Sandra is hesitant. Monique goes into the bathroom and steps into the shower. Moments later, she joins Monique. They scrub each others back with a shower brush, rinse off, step outside the shower and dry each other off. They return to the bedroom, get dressed hug and kiss then look at each other lovingly. "Time to go home," Sandra muses.

Back in her apartment, Sandra immediately notices that all of Chad's belongings are gone. She picks up Hope and kisses her. Spencer is asleep in bed, thumping his feet. Sandra shakes him awake. He sits up yawns and rubs his eyes. "Honey, I'm home. Where is Chad and all his belongings?" "He found a place to live he moved out early this morning. Did you and Monique have a good time?" he jokes. "We certainly did. You know she's my best friend." "Chad sends you his love." "That's nice of him. I see he must have cooked a farewell meal. The kitchen is a mess." "Yes, and it was delicious," Spencer says as he lets out a long fart. Sandra puts her hand over her nose. "Pardon me," Spencer says. "I have work to do," Sandra goes into the living room. Spencer stays in the bedroom.

Sandra goes through boxes of Eugene's files. The phone rings. "Hey, Monique. Everything is fine here. Chad moved out this morning." Holding the phone on her shoulder, she pulls out a file folder from the box. "I just found a copy of a Business Plan." She flips through the pages. "It's about 20 pages. I'll start on the Proposal now. See you later. I'll be here all day." Sandra hangs up the phone, goes to the kitchen and begins washing dishes. Spencer, she yells, "did Chad pay you your money? "No," he shouts. "He said he'd pay me next week." "Right, fat chance," Sandra yells.

After cleaning the kitchen, Sandra takes the copy of the Business Plan and goes to her laptop. She reads several pages, then turns on her computer, as she lights a cigarette. She thinks a minute then types the title page. *The Road To Success With Ivory Advertising Agency.* She says it out loud."The Road To Success With Ivory Advertising Agency." She takes out a notepad and makes a list. Let's see now, first we do a synopsis and or a background of the agency, bios of corporate officers, the staff and a description of past and current client list." The phone rings. She answers, "Ivory Advertising, Hello Mr. Duffy. Thank you for calling. Yes, we can deliver a sample copy. I am also working on a business plan to bring you up to date on our future strategies. You will have it in 10 business days. Call me if you have any questions."

Spencer walks into the room. "So now we're Ivory Advertising?" "I am not you. And this location is only for the time being." He sits down beside her and starts knocking his knees together. "You're really serious about reopening the ad agency aren't you." "It never closed. Just went on vacation as a Memorial to Eugene, Any way what do you expect me to do? During the middle of every month all I hear from you is that you're broke." The phone rings, "Ivory Advertising," Sandra answers. "Hello, Thomas. I'd be happy to meet you for lunch. The *Gigolo* at 12:30. You got it." "I have an appointment with a prospective investor." "Yeah, your last husband's best friend."

"That he was and now I hope he's going to help me and be my best friend," Sandra explains. Please call me a taxi on your phone. "I'm going to change. We will discuss my plans later." "I have to talk to you. "About what?" The Doctor's office called. They found cancerous tissue on my left ear. They want to remove it next week. It will be an out patient procedure, but someone has to be with me when I am released to go home. Monique has to be at the office to take care of business. I can ask Chad to do it again, but I would rather you come with me." "Of course, I will." "Thank you."Sandra walks over and hugs Spencer and kisses him on the cheek."

"I'll call the taxi," Spencer offers. Sandra takes her notepad, phone, the copy of the business plan and puts them in a leather portfolio. She goes into the bedroom. Hope follows her. "Hey, baby Mommy has to go out. But, we'll go for a walk when I get home." Sandra takes a puff from her inhaler, changes into a suave business suit, high heels and puts on complete make-up and oil sheen on her hair. "The taxi will be here in 10 minutes," Spencer shouts from the living room. "Thanks, again."

In the taxi, Sandra calls Monique. "Thomas asked me to lunch. I am on my way to the *Gigolo* to meet him. No, I'll handle it on my own. Haven't even smoked a cigarette. So, don't make me think about drugs and alcohol. It must be from that great massage I got last night. We're pulling up to the restaurant now. I'll call you after lunch." Sandra pays the taxi fare and goes inside the restaurant. Thomas is sitting at the bar. "My don't you look pretty," he says. "Our table is ready. I was having a martini while waiting for you." He escorts her to one of the best tables in the restaurant. Would you like a cocktail?" "I'll have a glass of Merlot." "Your wish is my command." A Server comes to the table hands them menus and Thomas orders the wine.

"The reason I wanted to see you Sandra, is that I am worried about your health and addictions. It is a big job to run a business whether it's large or small." "I know what you mean," Sandra interjects. Thomas goes on, "so your fitness is of great importance. I'd like to help you, not because I was Eugene's best friend but because I know you can do the job and keep the agency up and running."

"Thank you for your confidence. I have something to show you."

Sandra opens the portfolio and takes out the copy of the Business Plan and her notepad. "My guidelines for writing the Proposal is this Business Plan that Eugene wrote years ago for potential investors." I can upgrade it to the current date and Monique and I will present it to companies who are interested in working with us." I like the way you think," Thomas smiles. Let's order lunch he goes on.

Over lunch, Sandra explains her dilemma about COPD. "It is an incurable disease that I still can't believe I have." "Could it have happened from drug use?" Thomas asks. "The Doctor said it was from cigarette smoking. I am going to try to stop. Not just cigarettes, but everything else." "That brings up my other concern, Thomas admits, "a life insurance policy for you." "Most companies will not accept you if you have COPD or other ailments. I am not saying I cannot get you a policy. As I told you before I can and I will, but it will be expensive." "Doesn't the cost depend on the coverage I choose?" Sandra asks. "Yes, what amount are you thinking of?" I thought 10 or 15 thousand would cover cremation. The rest would go to my son Joey and his family." "I'll check a few companies and let you know what's best for you."

"I've been truthful and honest with you Thomas. Now, I want you to know this, I only want one Investor in Ivory Advertising and that is you. I'd be willing to give up 30% of the shares in the business in exchange for your guidance and support." "Thank you for your faith in me," Thomas says. "I will always think of you as a dear friend and Advisor. I must tell you that I spoke to Mr. Duffy from Duffy Brothers Restaurants. I promised him a sample of a new fun and activity book in 10 business days." "Why did you do that?" Thomas queries.

Because the Artist and Printer said they would work with me at our cost to get the job done." "You can be a bitch on wheels, when you want to be." "It's not just that, I know we can do it." Sandra affirms. Would you like another glass of wine?" Thomas asks. "No thank you." "Good girl. I have another appointment anyway. Let me give you a ride home." "You have a car here?" "Just a rental. I drive a jag in Canada when the weather is nice and a Jeep during the winter. I'll let you know my decision about Ivory Advertising in a few days."

At the apartment, Hope runs outside when Sandra opens the door. Sandra chases her around the parking lot. "Hope come here. Please baby come to Mommy." Hope stops in the middle of the parking lot as a car drives in. Sandra runs after Hope shouting to the female driver, "Stop, stop." The driver stops and Hope runs to Sandra. She picks Hope up and goes to the car. "Thank you so much for stopping." The driver smiles and pulls into a parking space. Holding Hope, Sandra walks into the apartment. Spencer is nowhere to be found. "Okay, we're going for a walk," she tells Hope as she puts on her collar and lease. The phone rings, Ivory Advertising. "Hello Pedro. No not today. Oh well, call me back in half an hour. I m going to take Hope for a walk in the park." She leaves the apartment with Hope.

In the neighborhood park, Hope runs around the bench where Sandra is sitting. She lights a cigarette takes a puff, then takes out her phone and dials Monique's number. "Monique, I had a great meeting with Thomas. He is definitely interested in becoming an investor. And he's going to get me a insurance policy. In the meantime, Mr. Duffy wants to see a sample of the book. I promised it to him in 10 business days. "Frank, the Artist and George, our Printer are ready to get to work. We're meeting them at 9 tomorrow morning at Frank's house. He lives in suburban West Palm Beach. So, you should pick me up at 8. Bring your laptop so we can work on the Business Plan at the same time we're putting the book together. I'll bring a flash drive of a six-page story that Frank wrote just before Eugene died. It was never published." "I'll see you in the morning." Sandra throws the cigarette on the ground.

Just as Sandra puts her phone away, Pedro walks up behind her. "Hello, Lady." Sandra turns around. "Pedro what are you doing here?" "Thought I'd find you here when you said you were taking Hope for a walk." "I don't have any money to buy anything." "That's alright your credit is good with me." "As hard as it is for me to say, I am trying to stay clean and sober for a while." "Whoa, that's a surprise. Especially, since I got pure stuff today." "Maybe you didn't hear me. I do not want to buy anything. You've got lots of customers sell it to them." Sandra gets up and walks off with Hope.

The next morning, Sandra waits outside her apartment waiting for

Monique. "Come on Monique. Where are you?" Finally, Monique drives up and blows the horn. Sandra gets in the car. "The traffic is crazy this time of the morning, Monique states. "I know. But, we better take 95 to get there on time," Sandra suggests. They drive up to a closed wrought iron gate, a security guard opens his door. "We're here to see Frank Mason. The Guard nods his head, opens the gate and waves them through. Sandra looks around at the condo buildings. She sees Frank, a deeply tanned man in his 40's, waving them forward to a parking space. They park the car, take out their gear and follow Frank to his condo.

Inside, there is a drawing table which takes up most of the living room. In the corner is a large, colorful parrot sitting in his cage. Sandra introduces Frank to Monique, they shake hands. Frank hugs Sandra. "Frank, I am so glad to see you, and thanks for coming through. But, where's George?" "He'll be here he's running late. Come over to my drawing table and take a look at what I've started on." He shows Sandra the 4-color cover of a chubby young boy with a Mohawk hair cut wearing a cape with a big D in the center. The character is settling on the ground in the middle of a group of smiling kids. His dialogue balloon states "Big D is here for you." The title at the top of the page reads, *The Adventures of Big D.*

"On the inside of the front cover, we'll print letters from members of the club and a website address so they can chat online. Then with your help Sandra, we'll write the 6-page story. We'll also include in the book, a pen pal list, a coloring page, a cross word puzzle, a membership application on the inside back cover and the kids menu on the back cover." "Sounds great but it's not a total of 16 pages," Sandra says. "You're right it's not," Frank adds. Don't you think kids would want a membership application online? "Yes, and there will be one." "Glad to hear you say that. I think the website name should be KidsRtalking. com. On the inside back cover of the book with the regular member application we should explain what the website is all about and give them subjects to chat about online, like bullying, surviving divorce, and other subjects we think of every month," Sandra explains.

"Where can Monique set up her laptop?" "On the dining room table is fine." Monique walks over to the table takes out the Business Plan and gets to work on rewriting it. Sandra and Frank discuss the details of the work on the book. The doorbell rings. That must be George.

Frank opens the door and in walks George, a jolly looking man who looks like he's imitating Santa Claus. He has shoulder length gray hair and a full gray beard. "Glad you could make it", Sandra says hugging George."Me too," George chuckles. Sandra's phone rings, she excuses herself. "Ivory Advertising. I'm working with my team right now. You will? Oh, my goodness. You won't be sorry. I'll meet you at eight at the *Gigolo* for dinner with Monique. You want all of us to come? That will be four of us. Okay, we'll be there."

Sandra grins from ear to ear. "That was Thomas. He's going to accept my offer and wants all of us to join him for dinner tonight at eight. He said he wants to meet his new team." "That's great," George says. "Maybe he'll give us an advance to print the master copy of the book." "I'll ask him about it," Sandra notes."Right now, we have to get as much done as we can so we can show him tonight. You guys work on the book and I'll work with Monique on the Proposal I mean, Business Plan."

Sandra goes to the dining room table. "You know Monique, there's not much to change except the 30% we're asking from our investor. Thomas saw this Business Plan a few days ago. What he's buying into is our ability to follow through with what we promise our clients.""I know. I haven't changed much, just bringing it more up to date," Monique states. "Good. Because even though he's taking a chance on us I want us to have as much of the Presentation, we can organize today to show him. And keep in mind, we can also offer a lesser percentage to other prospective investors." "Why would you want to do that?" Monique questions. "Just to cover ourselves in case something happens with Thomas." "Smart thinking." "That comes from all those years of working with Eugene. He was truly my Mentor." Tears well in Sandra's eyes. "I miss him so much." "I know one thing he's very proud of you," Monique smiles.

"He won't be proud if we don't get down to business. Frank, on the inside cover just put letters page in different colored caps at the top of the page. We don't have the time to look through the letters file I have in storage. If it's alright with everyone, we'll skip lunch and work until seven. We're going to a fancy restaurant for dinner, and we all already look presentable. Monique and I just need to freshen up hair and make-up. Except, men do have to wear ties. So, Frank, please loan

George one of yours. Let's keep working. Monique. You know what you're doing so keep it up. Frank, let me sit next to you and George. George, did you bring the paper samples?" "Right here." George opens a folder and lays it on a table. Turn on the radio. We need some easy listening music." Frank turns the radio to a jazz station. The parrot starts to make tweeting sounds. "Can he talk?" Monique asks. "When he wants to." Frank laughs.

"I know we've always printed the book on newspaper stock. "Tell me what you think if it was laminated?" Sandra asks. "Too expensive," George notes. "Newspaper is still the cheapest and the best for this kind of publication." "We'll still ship 500 books per case," Sandra reminds them. " And ship by UPS, or FEDEX which ever is cheapest" Frank adds. "Got any coffee, Frank?" "Made a fresh pot before you came. Go in the kitchen and help yourself. Everything is on the counter." The group gathers in the kitchen. Sandra holds up her cup, "I propose a toast to the most loyal, creative and talented team in the world." They raise their cups then take a sip of coffee. Okay, kids its back to work. I have to call Andrew, our Accountant, he's back in town from New York tonight. He has to start a new set of books, design invoices and other necessary forms we need. Keep in mind, he spent 10 years working with Eugene so we can learn a lot from him. I'll call him in the morning. Let him know we're back on track."

Monique and Sandra drive up to the Valet parking entrance, Frank pulls in behind them and George pulls in behind Frank. They get out of their cars and walk into the Gigolo restaurant. Thomas is waiting for them in the foyer. He hugs and kisses Sandra. She introduces Frank and George. He shakes their hands and kisses Monique's hand. "I've reserved the Conference Room for us so we can relax and concentrate on our meeting. Follow me." They walk behind Thomas with self-assurance.

He sits at the head of the table, Sandra sits to his right, Monique to his left Frank and George sit across from each other beside Monique and Sandra. On the wood trimmed wall is a large white banner with black letters, **Congratulations To The Creative Team At Ivory Advertising Agency.** Everyone smiles at each other and at Thomas. "Thank you," Sandra gushes. "My pleasure. Let's order cocktails," Thomas says. "No, we'll do that later, he motions to a waiter who is standing by. Bring me a bottle of your best bubbly.

"While we're waiting, show me what I am getting into. Sandra takes his lead. "First, we wish to submit our Business Plan. Monique hands Thomas a double pocket folder. "We also included Letters of Recommendation and a few newspaper articles about Eugene and the corporation." "Then we have a Master copy of the fun and activity book." Frank passes the book to Sandra. She hands it to Thomas. "The main character is Big D. The permanent storyline is that he helps kids out of trouble from elementary to junior high school with a positive solution and image.

The inside front cover will be Letters to Big D. All letters sent to Big D will be answered with pre-printed letters from specific categories and sent once a week by third class mail. Topics will be such as coping with their personal problems, bullying and an array of subjects which are listed in the Business Plan. Thomas turns the page. Sandra goes on. "There will be a different 6 page adventure story every month. Then there's a coloring page and a pen pal page. The inside back cover has the Big D Club membership application and information about the website for online chatting. The back cover is the Kids Menu." When we receive member apps, the child will get an envelope with a Welcome Letter signed by Big D and a membership card.

The Waiter brings in the bottle and glasses. He pours the drinks. Thomas raises his glass. A toast to the future growth of Ivory Advertising Agency. They lift their glasses and sip. "Now, you've impressed me so far. However, I know you have to hire at least 2 or 3 people to help run the program." "You're right," Sandra, agrees. "We think college students, studying business, would be perfect." "Is Andrew still your Accountant?" "Yes, he's not here because he's in New York on business. He's returning tonight. "Let's order dinner, Thomas says. He motions to the Waiter who hands out menus. Order whatever you like, there is no cost to you. The team says thank you in unison.

After they order, Thomas asks what else he should know. Sandra explains in detail about the Duffy account. They are the one and only account. "I talked to Mr. Duffy several days ago and he wants to see the Business Plan and the master copy of the book. After that he'll make a decision." If I were you, Thomas suggests, I'd look for other clients immediately." "We're going too. Monique and I will start making appointments tomorrow." Who are you calling?" "Corporate headquarters of other restaurant chains." "You need an office." Their meals arrive. "If anyone wants wine with dinner, go ahead and order it, Thomas offers. Everyone declines.

"I have an idea," Thomas offers. There's a vacant office in the building where I have my insurance agency. Right next door as a matter of fact, in Boca Raton. I have office furniture in storage that I can loan to you. For the time being, all you need are your cell phones and laptops." "That's a long drive every day I live in Tequesta and Monique lives in Jupiter." "I can work at home," Frank says and "I have the print shop," George states. Sandra is speechless. "I don't know how to thank you." "Yes, you do. Get the Duffy account and move forward. Anyone want dessert?" Everyone shakes there heads no. "Frank and Sandra talk to the Attorney tomorrow. Call me when he or she can meet with me and my Attorney. I'll be here for another week. When we sign the paperwork for the shares I will have a cashier's check put into the ad agency account." "Do you mind my asking what that amount will be?" Monique asks. "It depends on how much the shares cost or what I decide to give the agency." Thomas turns to Sandra. "If you like I'll give you a ride home. I know it's been a long day for all of you and it's almost midnight." Thomas calls over the Waiter, "take the banner down. The banner is a gift for you Sandra." "Great, We'll hang it in our new office." Are we all ready?" Thomas asks. "Give me a minute? Sandra asks. "I'll join you," Monique says suspiciously. The women walk to the Ladies Room. "I need to take a puff of my inhaler," Sandra tells Monique. "Having trouble breathing." "Thank God. You scared me, Monique smiles. "No, my dear no, drugs." Sandra takes out her inhaler and takes a puff. "Okay, let's join the boys."

As Sandra and Monique walk out of the Ladies Room, the men are waiting for them in the foyer. Thomas hands Sandra the folded banner. "Don't worry about the Valet," Thomas tells them. "I've already taken care of him." The group goes out to their waiting cars. "Don't forget," Sandra, reminds them. "We're meeting at Frank's house at 8 tomorrow morning." They nod their heads and wave good-bye. Sandra gets in Thomas' car and they drive off.

In the car, Thomas asks if Sandra wants to go anywhere else before he drops her off. She explains that she's had enough excitement for the evening, and gives him directions to her apartment. She tells him again, how grateful she is with his assistance. "It's all because I know it's a business that will profit," Thomas responds. "And I am happy to see you making an effort to stay clean and sober." I was sober for 2 years, but at that time, I did it on my own. "You are never on your own. God is always with you. I admire you for your determination." "I'm going to start going to evening meetings, Sandra promises. Thomas pulls his car in front of her apartment building. He hands her the banner and kisses her on the cheek. "Call me when you finish work tomorrow." "Done deal," Sandra says as she gets out of the car.

Inside the empty apartment, Hope runs around Sandra's legs, wagging her tail. "Hey, Mommy's baby, are you hungry? Hope barks. Sandra prepares Hope's food dish and puts fresh water in her bowl. She sits on the sofa and lays back her head with a smile on her face. The phone rings. "Hello, Pedro. No, I'm still interested, but not right now. Please, understand I have a lot of responsibility. I'm serious. People are depending on me. Spencer walks in the door in his sloppy jeans and wrinkled shirt. He stops outside before he closes the door. "I have to go," Sandra hangs up the phone.

"You're home early," Sandra says in surprise. Spencer sits next to her. "I guess you forgot. I have to be at the Out patient center in the morning," Spencer says. "Oh gosh, I did forget. What time do you have to be there?" "At 7, Chad is driving us." Sandra calls Monique. "Hi, it's me. Spencer has his surgery in the morning. I have to go with him. Yeah, I forgot. Some how I'll get to Frank's in the afternoon. Then you can give me a ride home. Okay? Thanks Babe." "I'm going to bed. I am really tired, Spencer yawns. "Me too. Let's go," Sandra takes Spencer's hand. Sandra calls to Hope, "Come on Baby, it's time for bed." They walk to the bedroom.

Sandra watches television in the waiting room of the out patient center. She takes out her inhaler and takes a puff. She coughs then takes another puff. Chad joins her. "When are you going to pay Spencer the money you stole from him?" "Please, don't be upset with me Miss Sandra. I told Spencer I should have enough to pay him by the first of the month." "Are you still working as a Courier for that so called company in Alabama?" Yes, they told me I can make up to $1,500.00

a month," he says proudly. "Yeah right," Sandra replies. "All I know, is that it sounds like you're picking up dirty money and sending it to some crooks." "Don't worry, Miss Sandra everything is working out fine." Spencer is pushed into the room in a wheelchair by a nurse. He looks tired and dopey. "I am ready to go," he announces. "Let's get you home," Sandra, offers. "You look a mess." "I feel fine. I think I'll even go to work tonight," Spencer murmurs. Chad holds Spencer's arm, Sandra holds the other arm. "No work for you. It's home to bed," she says sharply. "Chad go get the car." Chad leaves. "Let's go outside and wait for him. There's a bench at the entrance." They get outside just as Chad drives up. Sandra opens the door.

At the apartment, Spencer is asleep in bed Sandra covers him with a blanket. Hope sits next to Sandra wagging her tail. She goes to the living room, puffs on her inhaler, picks up the phone and dials. "Monique, I can't get to Frank's, I'd rather stay here and watch over Spencer, like I promised. Call me tonight when you get home." Sandra picks up Hope and strokes her back. Hope gives her a doggy grin. Then Sandra calls Thomas. "Hi, it's me. I couldn't go to work today. My friend Spencer had minor surgery. I have to stay here and watch over him. He'll be fine. He said he wanted to go to work tonight. I don't think that would be safe or that he can slide down that pole. I thought you knew. He is a male stripper. You sound like everybody else. Yes, I know I can do better. Spencer came into my life, when I was lonely and depressed. Plus, he's been clean and sober for years. Okay, I'll see you in the morning for breakfast. We don't have a car. Can you pick me up at eight?" Sandra hangs up the phone picks up Hope. She goes in the bedroom, where she and Hope lay down besides Spencer and fall asleep.

At the One Bite Café in Palm Beach, Thomas and Sandra eat breakfast."I left Spencer a note before I left, so he knows I won't be back for a while," Sandra grins. "Have you found an Attorney?" "Yes, I have several that I'd like to interview. One is in Boca Raton. I don't know how far he's away from the office. And the team wants to know when we can move in." "That's one of the reasons I invited you to breakfast. The space I thought was empty has been rented," Thomas says in disappointment. "Oh, no" Sandra moans. "What are we going to do?" "Well, I've been thinking about that. For the time being, you and Monique can use the conference room in my office until we find another space. That way you'll have a place to meet your prospective clients. I'll even let you put the Ivory Advertising banner on the wall." "You'd do that for us?" Sandra says in appreciation. "I told you before and I tell you again. I'm your friend and I'll do what ever I can to help you." "Thank you my dear," Sandra hugs Thomas. "I have a morning meeting to go to. Would you drop me off?" "My pleasure," Thomas says.

Sandra sits in a small room full of people. The Male Moderator tells them that the subject for the day is "Disbelief." He speaks a few minutes about what it means to lie to ones self. "First understand that we are alcoholics. Once you do that, you will better understand how not to relapse," he goes on. "We will be recovering for the rest of our lives. We suffer from an incurable disease. You are here by the grace of God. It's his leadership that will take you down the road of recovery." He looks around the room. "Let's share a few stories about disbelief." He looks at Sandra. "You're new here. Do you have anything to share so we can get to know you better?"

Sandra clears her throat. "Hi, my name is Sandra. It has taken me a long time to believe that I have a drug and alcohol problem. I convinced myself that there was no way I would be considered in life in such a negative way. I have been sober off and on for 2 years, but I secretly relapse whenever I can because of a sometime boring life. The worst thing I hate about being sober is gaining weight." The crowd applauds, Sandra smiles. "This time around by the grace of God, I truly want to make it work. Thank you." The crowd echoes, "Thank you Sandra."

Monique and Sandra sit in a booth at the *Hideaway*. Country and Western music is playing in the background. They both drink sodas. "At first, I was nervous, then I spoke from my heart. What an amazing relief," Sandra tells Monique. Her phone rings, "Hi Dina. Hold on, I can't hear you I m in a noisy restaurant, okay bar." Sandra steps outside. "He did what? Where is he now? Is he going to be okay?" "I'll try to get there. Tell Joey how much I love him." Sandra hangs up the phone and calls Thomas. "Hi, I have an emergency. My son Joey took an overdose of pills today and he's in the hospital. Can I ask you to buy me a round trick ticket to New York? As soon as I can. They pumped out his stomach, his wife Dina says he is barely alive. Okay, please call me back. I am at the *Hideaway* with Monique."

Sandra makes her way back to the booth. She's crying. "That was

Dina, Joey's wife. He tried to kill himself this afternoon." "Why?" Monique asks. "I don't know it could be because he lost his job. He has a lot of pride." "I called Thomas and he said he'd buy me a plane ticket."Why did you call him instead of asking Spencer. He doesn't have that kind of money in hand. He doesn't even have a checking or saving account. This is too unbelievable. I need a drink." "Are you crazy? No you don't. You just went to your first meeting today and now you want a drink?" I cannot help myself. I need something to calm me down.

She pushes her way through the crowd to the bar. She gets the Owner's attention. "Hi, Nick. Give me a double shot of rum and coke." She lights a cigarette. "Where have you been hiding, Lady?" Nick asks. "Busy, with my work. I'll tell you about it later. She downs the drink at the bar, leaving Monique sitting at the booth. "Give me another," Sandra asks Nick. She takes money out of her purse and pays the bill. "Send another over to the booth in about 5 minutes." "Here, I'll make it for you now. I'm short on Wait staff." Nick hands the drinks to Sandra.

Sandra takes the drinks over to the booth. Monique is upset. "What are you doing to yourself? Monique asks. "Getting ready for the worse," Sandra cries. "You're all ready making it worse. How are we going to keep a struggling business going without you here. I am depending on you. I won't be gone that long." "How do you know?" You're right I don't." "Let's just say I'll stay for 3 days or a week at the most." Sandra takes out her inhaler and puffs twice. She then lights a cigarette.

Monique shakes her head. "This is how you handle having COPD?" "Don't worry, I'll stop." "All you're doing is lying to yourself. You need to see a Shrink." "I've given up most of my career to work with you and this is what I get in return." "Please understand," Sandra cries. "I love you." "I love you too more than you know," Monique asserts. They clasp each others hands, just as Thomas arrives at the booth. "I thought I should come over and let you know what I've arranged." "Yes. Please sit down," Sandra says wiping her eyes. Thomas reaches in his pocket and gives Sandra a wad of bills. "Here

Is eight hundred dollars, I made a reservation for a round trip ticket from here to New York and back.

Your flight leaves at nine in the morning, I'll pick you up at six in the morning and take you to the airport. We have to pick up the ticket at the airport. I left the return trip open. The rest of the money is yours to use for petty cash." I don't know how I can thank you," Sandra cries. "I do," Thomas says. "Monique would you excuse us?" he asks, "You bet your life. I am going home. Have fun, kids." Thomas takes Sandra's hand and they walk out with Monique. Sandra and Thomas wave good-bye to Monique as they get in his car. He pulls Sandra over to him and kisses her passionately. "I am tired of waiting, Sandra. I have wanted you for a long time. Come home with me." Sandra agrees, and they speed off.

At Thomas' penthouse, Sandra and Thomas run inside acting like teenagers. He goes into the bedroom, ripping off his clothes along the way, she runs behind."Come into my arms my darling." Sandra hugs him and they fall on the bed together. She takes off her shirt and skirt. He removes her bra and panties. Huffing and puffing they kiss each others bodies. Thomas jumps on top of Sandra. She entwines her legs around his neck. He enters his long, large, hard penis inside her. She screams with pleasure. Thomas makes hard, passionate love to her. Within minutes, he let's out a loud groan and has a body quaking organism. They are both breathless. Thomas comes to his senses. "Okay, girlfriend, we have to get you home so you can get ready for your flight." "Shit, I wish I had my clothes here. I want to spend the night with you." "Not this time. You have a lot on your plate. Get dressed. I'll take you home."

Thomas pulls his car in the parking lot of Sandra's apartment building. He kisses her, she gets out of the car and waves good-bye. Sandra walks into an empty apartment. Spencer is at work. Hope runs up to her with her tail wagging. "Hello, baby, she says as she rubs Hope's back. She goes to the bedroom takes out her suitcase and begins to pack. She starts coughing. She reaches for her inhaler on the bedside table and takes two puffs. She chokes and sits down on the side of the bed, takes a few deep breaths and relaxes. Her body shivers as she thinks about her episode with Thomas. She finishes packing, takes off her clothes, puts Hope on the bed and then goes to bed. She immediately falls asleep with Hope in her arms.

In the morning, before daylight, Sandra wakes up Spencer. "I have to go to New York," she tells him."Joey tried to kill himself. He's in the hospital. Spencer sits up."I m sorry, Sandra. Do you need Chad to pick you up?" "No, Thomas is taking me to the airport and paying for the ticket. He should be here any minute." A car horn is blown. "That's him. I will call you. Take good care of Hope." Sandra picks up her luggage and heads for the door. At the airport, Sandra gets out of the car, blows Thomas a kiss and goes into the terminal.

In New York, Dina picks Sandra up at the airport. " Why would he do such a thing?" Sandra asks. "His Doctor prescribed pills for knee pain. He liked them so much he started taking them day and night. It's his way of escaping reality. He doesn't know I called you." "Why not?" Sandra says amazed. "He's to upset with himself. He doesn't even want me at the hospital or to see Chloe." "And how is Chloe?" "She's confused about seeing her Dad on the bathroom floor. She thought he was asleep." "Where is she?" "With my Mother." "Well, let's go to the hospital now." Sandra orders. "That's where we're off to." Dina turns the car into the hospital parking lot. They go into the hospital to Joey's room. He's asleep.

Sandra holds his hand bows her head in prayer and begins to cry. Joey wakes up. He looks at Sandra. "I am sorry Mom. I tried to do it the right way." "What do you mean, son?" "I didn't swallow enough pills to die.?" Joey whispers. "Stop being silly. You are as bad as I am." Sandra responses. "Stop hating yourself, and take responsibility." "I can't find a job, Dina's family has been helping us out." "You've got a job if you want it. Come to Florida and work with me." "That's to far away from my family." "Have you forgotten? I am also your family. Bring Dina and Chloe with you." "I think that's a great idea Sandra. But what would he do?" Dina inquires. "Be Office Manager of Ivory Advertising. Eugene left the company to me. We're reopening with the help of his best friend Thomas." "I remember him, Joey smiles. I thought he was dead." "Well, he isn't. He's very much alive and owns thirty percent of the company" Sandra replies. "To tell you the truth, Dina, adds, Joey and I could use a break. We haven't been getting along lately." "I'm not happy to hear that," Sandra sighs. "I'll give you two some privacy and let you talk about my offer." Sandra walks out of the room.

Outside the hospital, Sandra lights a cigarette and removes her cell phone from her purse. She takes a quick puff, throws the cigarette on the ground and dials Thomas' number. "Hi, Thomas. I miss you too. He's going to be all right. I offered him a job as Office Manager for us.

He can stay at my apartment, until he finds a place of his own. Dina likes the idea. They haven't been getting along lately. He'd make a good Manager. He was with the Loan Company three years before they down sized the staff and moved to Manhattan, I will be home in three days. I have already made my reservation. I will use the rest of the money to buy a one -way ticket for Joey if he accepts. Is that all right with you? Thank you."

Sandra walks back into Joey's hospital room. Dina and Joey are arguing. "You prick," Dina shouts. She will never forget seeing you laying on the floor passed out. I should have listened to my Mother, and not marry you." "I've been doing the best I can, Dina." "No you haven't." "I've waited for years to see you find a career to mirror your education." "That's hard for me to do when we live in the woods and drive a broken down old car." Joey claims. Sandra walks further into the room. "Hey, you two, what's going on, I could hear you shouting from down the hall." "We're discussing our future, Mom. Maybe, I should take your suggestion." Joey glares at Dina.

A few days later, the team from Ivory Advertising, including Joey, sit in the conference room at Thomas' office. The Ivory Advertising Agency banner hangs on the wall. Sandra speaks first. "Mr. Duffy will be here at three o'clock. So we better get organized. Let's talk about his company believing enough in us to continue to be a client. We will introduce Thomas as our new Investor, then Thomas will explain his background and why he is investing in us. After that, Frank will show the *Adventures of Big D* prototype, and describe it from cover to cover. George, will discuss the use of newspaper print and why it is the best paper for the publication. Andrew is our Accountant."

"Joey is our new Office Manager, and oversees the daily routine of our operation. Monique is working on a Marketing and Sales Proposal for the Duffy Brothers, to show them how the characters from the book can become plush toys, a piggy bank and or a baseball cap with the *Big D* insignia on the top front center. All the aforementioned would be sold at the restaurants. We still have to get the cost for these products by first designing them then decide what the costs and materials will be. Andrew will help with that. So, Frank will work closely with Monique and me so we can discuss the details in a timely fashion." Frank and Monique smile at each other.

The presentation to the Duffy Brothers was a complete success. It was decided that the fun and activity book will be ready for shipment in thirty days. Sandra is extremely happy, as is everyone else.

After, Mr. Duffy leaves, Sandra suggests that they go the *Hideaway* to celebrate. Thomas declares that, even though he does not like the place he'll buy the drinks. Everyone arrives at the designation in their cars. Joey rides with Monique. Sandra is in the car with Thomas.

At the *Hideaway*, the group of six takes charge of a large table in the back of the bar. Sandra excuses herself and goes to the Ladies Room. Inside, she finds a woman in her 30's crying. "What's the problem?" Sandra asks. "I just found out that my girlfriend is sleeping with another woman." The woman wails. Sandra hugs the woman, "Do you love this woman with your heart of hearts?" "Yes, we've been together for three years. How could she do this to me?" "There's always a reason," Sandra explains. Sandra takes out her inhaler and puffs. "What is that for? You have any drugs?" The woman asks. "I have COPD, the inhaler medicine helps keep my lungs clear and no I do not have any drugs. Take care of yourself" Sandra smiles and walks out.

When Sandra returns to the table, Joey walks up to her. "Mom, I have some questions to ask you." "Yes son what is it?" Sandra asks. "I don't understand why you like this place. Everyone in here is what we call in New York a redneck." "No they're not." "But, the only music they play on the jukebox is country and western." "That doesn't make them rednecks. I like it here because it's close to home and everyone loves me. I know it's a little strange for us to be the only people of color here but that's just the way it is tonight. All the bars in this area are like this." Haven't you noticed? We live in a predominately white neighborhood. And you are in Florida not New York. Here, take my credit card and play some music you'd like to hear and have a good time" Sandra pats Joey on the back. "Thanks Mom." Joey makes his way pass the bar to the jukebox. Sandra sits next to Monique. "There was a lesbian in the Ladies Room crying about losing her girlfriend." "What a shame. I know how she feels," Monique whispers. "How would you know?" Sandra asks in dismay. "We can talk about it when we're alone," Monique offers.

One of Joey's Motown selections from the jukebox begins playing. Thomas asks Sandra to dance. She gets up and they dance next to a pool table. Thomas holds her close as slow jazz plays. "When can I see you again?"Thomas asks. You're looking at me right now, Sandra teases. "You know what I mean." Sandra kisses him on the cheek. "Of course I do. I'm sorry." "I have to work things out. With Joey staying at the apartment I don't want him to think something is going on with us. His respect is very important to me. As you know, it would be easier with us to see each other since Spencer works at night." "Have you asked Joey if he wants to see Mr. Mighty Ram perform? Yes, and he refused the offer. He can't even believe that I am living with a male stripper." "Neither can, I" Thomas asserts. "Okay let's go back to the table. I want to see you just as much as you want to see me. I promise we will work something out this week." Sandra says lovingly. They walk to the table as Joey asks a woman to dance with him. Sandra smiles, it happens to be the woman Sandra talked to in the Ladies Room.

Thomas announces that he is tired and he excuses himself after kissing Sandra and Monique on the cheek. "Thank you again, for doing such a great job with the Duffy Brothers. I know there's more to come. He shakes hands with Frank and George. See you tomorrow," he says as he leaves. Frank and George laud Sandra's performance at the meeting, She laughingly says, "Well I've been known as a bitch on wheels. "And that you are," Frank adds. "But, I couldn't be one without you guys." Sandra starts moving erotically as a popular Motown record plays. Come on let's dance before we leave. They all get up and dance, Joey joins them. Sandra twirls around Monique and Joey. Frank and George go back to the table. The trio keeps dancing. "How many records did you play"? Sandra asks Joey. "This is the last one," Joey yells. The music stops and everyone joins Frank and George. They all say their good-byes and walk to their cars.

The next morning, Spencer and Sandra are arguing in the bedroom. "When you moved in here, you said you would pay the rent. The Landlord called me and said we're two months behind. What's wrong with you? I put up with your sloppy, messy ways and lack of concern about our future. All you can think about is how many cigarettes I smoke in a day. I am sick of you. What happened to the rent money?" Joey sits on the sofa listening to the confrontation. It reminds him of Sandra's arguments with his father. He picks up Hope holds her to his chest and strokes her back. Sandra enters the living room. Spencer stays in the bedroom. She looks distraught and unhappy. She tells Joey it is time to get dressed for work and that he can use the bathroom first. Joey smiles and goes into the bathroom.

In the conference room of Thomas' office, Sandra gives her team, Monique and Frank their assignments for the day. However, she's at a loss as to what Joey can do. She scratches her forehead in earnest. Monique makes a suggestion, "Let's make this his training period. He can spend time with each of us to see and understand what our jobs are." "That's a good idea," Sandra agrees. "Joey get a pad, so you can take notes." "Here, I have one," Monique gives Joey a pad and pen. "Great," Sandra smiles. "Joey today you'll work with Frank. We have to get the book layout to George in a few days. He's waiting at his shop to start printing. Thomas and I have an appointment this afternoon so I won't be here. Thomas will take me home, Monique, will you drop Joey off at home?" Monique nods with a sly grin. Thomas enters the room, are you ready Sandra?" Yes, I'll be right with you. I'll meet you in the car." Sandra goes to the bathroom, takes a puff from her inhaler, smoothes her hair and puts on lipstick. Sandra wishes everyone good luck with their assignments and tells them to call her if they have any questions.

Once in the car, Sandra hugs and kisses Thomas. "That appointment idea was brilliant," she muses. "When I want something, I aim to get it. Besides it's been two weeks since we were together." Thomas jokes. "I know I miss you," Sandra whispers licking his cheek. Thomas drives in to the garage of his building. Okay, my sweet, we're here. They get out of the car and take the elevator to the penthouse.

Sandra hugs and kisses him in the elegant living room. He leads her to the bedroom. They sit on the side of the bed and kiss while slowly removing each other's clothes. They fall back on the bed. "Okay sweetheart here's what we asked for," he proclaims while rubbing his penis back and forth. "Have you ever had it backwards?" he asks. "What do you mean?" "In the ass." he says impatiently. Sandra frowns. "No, and I don't want too." "I promise you'll like it." "That's not true. You like it otherwise you wouldn't ask me to do it." "Okay, at least I tried." Thomas jumps on top of Sandra. She holds her legs up in the air, he enters his hard penis inside her. She moans while he thrushes in and out of her. Thomas keeps going as Sandra pleas, "not so hard, that hurts."

Thomas takes his time with having a climax. "Squeeze my balls," he orders Sandra. "I can't reach them," she moans.

Thomas removes his penis lays back on the bed and starts to masturbate. "Squeeze my balls now," he orders. Sandra does what he asks. He let's out a loud groan and has a organism which shoots all over his stomach. "Get me a wash cloth from the bathroom," he says breathlessly. Sandra gets up, goes to the bathroom and comes back with a wet wash cloth. "Well, I'm glad you're happy," Sandra says in disgust. "Please, take me home. I need to be alone." "What about Spencer and Joey?" Thomas asks. "Joey's still at the office and Spencer is at the *Mandarin* putting together a new show." "Okay, let's get dressed and go." "I have to go back to the office. What do you want me to tell your team?" "The truth. Tell them you took me home." Sandra laughs.

In her empty apartment, Sandra sits on the sofa and takes a puff from her inhaler. She throws Hope's favorite toy across the room. Hope fetches it and brings it back. After several minutes of play, Sandra lights a cigarette, gets up and surveys the room. It is a disaster. Old newspapers, unopened mail, empty coffee cups and dirty plates lay everywhere. Sandra shakes her head in sadness. She gets a plastic garbage bag from the kitchen where the waste basket overflows with garbage. Slowly, she begins cleaning the apartment. The door opens. It's Joey. "Hi Mom, why didn't you come back to the office." "I am tired sweetheart," Sandra says. "Well, it sure wasn't the same without you there." "I take that as a compliment. Thank you" "You want me to take Hope for a walk to the park?" "That would be nice. She hasn't been outside for a long time." Joey puts on Hope's collar and leash and leaves. Sandra's phone rings.

"Hi Monique. What's the good news? You're kidding. Please pick me up so we can talk about it. Call me from the parking lot when you get here. I don't want you to see what disarray this place is that I call home. I'm so embarrassed that Joey is here in this mess." Sandra hangs up the phone and continues cleaning. The phone rings again. "Hi Pedro. Thank you for your patience. No, I've just been smoking cigarettes. No pills either. I know it's been about six weeks." "Since the last time I saw you, I went to a meeting and shared my problems with drinking and drugs." Joey opens the door with Hope in his arms. "Okay I have to go now, my son just came home. Yes, he's living with us until he finds a place of his own. Don't worry I'll stay in touch." Sandra puts the phone in her purse. "Hey, honey. Did Hope do all her business?" "Sure did." A horn blows. "Sweetie that must be Monique. We're going to have a discussion about a new client." The horn is blown again. "Would you finish emptying the garbage?" "Sure Mom, no problem." Sandra blows him a kiss and heads for the door.

In Monique's car, Sandra begins to cry as she lights a cigarette. "I am sick and tired of that idiot, Spencer. What was I thinking when I told him he could move in with me? He's disgusting. I thought I could help him change his ways. But, he's never going to change to be the kind of man I want in my life. He likes living in the dark. He always wants the hurricane shutter closed on our bedroom window. He never wants the light on. He says he doesn't like light because his eyes are photo sensitive. He only has sight in his left eye. And I am sick of him asking me how many cigarettes I've smoked every day" "He's just looking out for your good health. What has he done this time?" Monique asks. "First of all he hasn't paid the rent for two months. He's been betting all his money on the horses. I had no idea. I don't have enough money from my Widow's Benefits to pay the rent. I don't want to be evicted. And I am not going to ask Thomas for a loan. Spencer should move to OHIO." Monique pulls the car into the *Hideaway* parking lot. "I have good news for you, which might help solve your problem," Monique says slyly.

The women go to a booth and sit down. Smooth jazz music is playing softly in the background A Waiter comes over to take their order. "I'll have ginger ale with a water back", Sandra orders as she lights a cigarette. Monique claps her hands ."At least you're not drinking." "Give me a draft beer," Monique states. "So what's the good news?" Sandra asks. "If you remember, I've been talking to the Brill Company about a brochure for their tile and floor products. The owner of the company called when you were with Thomas and said they'd like to see a layout for the brochure." "That's marvelous," Sandra smiles.

Frank started working on it right away." "He shouldn't have done that. The Duffy Brothers come first." "We know. Frank was just throwing some ideas around with me about the wording in the brochure. We think there should be 4-color pictures of the high end products and we can create a logo and a slogan. They've been in business over twenty years and have six locations throughout the state," Monique shares.

Sandra downs her ginger ale and lights another cigarette. "When are you going to stop smoking?" Monique asks. "I can't stop everything all at once," Sandra claims. She waves to the Waiter, he comes to the booth. "Another ginger ale and draft beer."

"So, what's your idea about the rent?" Sandra asks. "We can ask the Brill Company for an advance. How much rent do you owe?" "The rent is $700 a month." "We can ask them for a thousand and I'll loan you the rest. Have you ever thought Spencer has these problems from being in the army for six years?" "I don't know." "He won't get help," Sandra cries. "His voice is even changing, he grumbles so much I can't even understand what he's saying." "How can we ask for an advance without being found out?" "You and I will make an appointment with the Owner of the company show him the layout of the brochure and ask for the advance." "You think it will work?" Sandra asks. "Let's pray that it does. I'll create an invoice for a Security Fee as an advance and we will also give him a contract from Ivory Advertising to administer the job within a certain period of time." "I love the way you think, Monique, always have." Sandra says with admiration.

At the Brill Company 10 days later, Sandra and Monique sit in the Waiting Room. They are dressed in their Sunday best, with perfect make-up and hair styles. Monique looks like the fashion model she is and Sandra is close behind with her business attire of a pin stripe suit. A Secretary comes out of an office, "Mr. Brill will see you now." Sandra and Monique walk into a lavish office of wood walls and marble floor. Mr. Brill sits behind a large antique oak desk. The 60 something year old man, is dressed in a expensive suit with a vest and tie. "Welcome ladies, he says. "I didn't expect such a charming duo." "Thank you," Sandra responses. "And we want you to know we have your best interest at heart." Monique adds.

Sandra opens a portfolio and takes out the layout of the brochure. She hands it to Mr. Brill. "The blank squares are where photos of rooms and offices where your product was used will be inserted. A photo of your office would be perfect for the front cover. And at the top of the page will be a custom designed logo and slogan below it." Do you have any clients that would allow us to take photos in both home and office?" Monique asks. "Yes, I do." We have a professional photographer on staff that will take the photos." Sandra adds. "You will approve and choose the negatives before placing them in the brochure." "Sounds good so far," Mr. Brill states. "When do you want the product to be finished?" Sandra asks. "Let's say the next thirty to sixty days." "How many do you want?" "One million to start," Mr. Brill answers. Monique and Sandra look at each other and smile. Sandra goes on, "The brochure should be laminated, if that's all right with you," Monique states. "By all means," Mr. Brill agrees. Sandra takes out a double pocket folder. "In case you wanted to know more about Ivory Advertising, we prepared this presentation for you." Sandra hands the folder to Mr. Brill. "It contains letters of commendation about our agency and a list of our clients, which include the Duffy Brothers." "I know who they are," Mr. Brill says in surprise. "I've eaten at one of their restaurants."

"In order for us to get started on the job, we always ask new clients for a security fee. We're serious about you. But, we want you to be serious about us." Sandra admits. "We also ask that you sign a contract for the job." Monique adds. She hands the contract to Mr. Brill. "The security fee is one thousand dollars." "When is that due?" Mr. Brill asks. "Today, if possible." Sandra notes. Not so fast Ladies. First, I want my Attorney to read the contract. If all is in order, you'll receive the security fee along with the signed contract. Give me a few days and I'll have my secretary call you. It was nice meeting you. Mr. Brill escorts Sandra and Monique out of the office.

In Monique's car, Sandra shakes her head in frustration. "I really thought we had him," she wails. "We do. He just needs time to think it over." Monique says. "You really think so?" "Yes, I've met many men like him. Don't you get the picture? He was dressed the way he was only for our meeting. He's probably heard about the new President of Ivory Advertising, and what a hot lady she is. He will keep us hanging until he really has his Attorney look at the contract. I am glad we copied one of Eugene's old contracts to give him." "But, he might be checking out other companies besides us," Sandra laments. "Of course he is. But, we're the best," Monique glows.

Back at the office, Sandra and Monique sit in the conference room with Joey, George and Frank. Monique is telling them what a good job Sandra did with Mr. Brill. "And he wants one million copies of the brochure," she adds. The men applaud. Sandra cuts in, "Monique wasn't to bad her self. It was truly a team effort." Joey asks Sandra if he can speak to her privately. "Yes, my dear. Let's go outside." They walk out of the office to the patio. "Mom I need to go back home. I spoke to Dina and she misses me." "I am sure she does." Sandra comments. "Not only that, she's pregnant," Joey smiles. Congratulations my son." I'm so happy Mom. I don't belong here. I'm going to find a job close to home. I'll even work where ever I can as long as it's close to my family." When do you want to leave?" "By the end of the week." "We'll make your reservation right now." They walk back to the office.

At the airport, Sandra and Thomas walk to the passenger gate with Joey. He is close to tears from confusion. "Calm down, my son." Sandra says. "You're doing the right thing." "I want to believe that," Joey says with a frown on his face. Put a smile on that face and go home to your family." Joey gives Sandra a long bear hug. They cry in each others' arms. Thomas separates them. "Come on you two, this is supposed to be a celebration. Joey you're just a phone call away from your Mother." "You're right, sir. I'll call you every Sunday, Mom. Just like I used too." Sandra smiles and holds his cheeks between her hands. Joey shakes Thomas' hand. "I've learned a lot from you, thank you." Thomas hugs Joey. "I think of you as the son I never had." Joey waves good-bye and walks through the gate.

As Thomas and Sandra drive from the airport, Sandra tries to keep from crying. "Damn, I'm messing up my eye make-up." She laughs tearfully. "You can always replace that but you cant replace a child."

"Do you have children?" "No, unfortunately my wife died in childbirth." "Oh, Thomas I' am so sorry." "It was years ago but I will never forget it. She was extremely beautiful and had the best personality. Some what like yours. People loved her." "How long were you married?" "Ten of the best years of my life. I had just started the insurance company." "And you never remarried?" "Don't want too." Thomas pulls into the garage of his building. "Hey, wait a minute, Sandra exclaims, I'm not in the mood for that. Besides, I have a headache, I want to get back to the office." "Well, I am not going to beg." He makes a u turn and drives out of the garage. "Thank you," Sandra whispers.

Thomas drives into the parking lot of his office. Sandra get out of the car and walks to the conference room. Monique is alone talking on the telephone. She waves to Sandra. "Yes, Mr. Duffy, your book will be ready for your approval in a few days. Frank, our Artist is working on the layout day and night. Sandra sits next to Monique. She looks wane and distraught. Monique gives her a worried look. "Don't forget, I'll have Sandra call you in a few days." Monique hangs up the phone. "Are you all right?" Monique asks. "I don't know." Sandra replies. Then without notice, Sandra closes her eyes and has a seizure. Monique calls 911, and screams for Thomas to come into the room.

In the hospital Emergency Room, Sandra is in bed asleep. The Doctor is talking to Monique. "Your friend has a seizure disorder that can be controlled with medication." She can go home when she wakes up." I am awake," Sandra mumbles. The Doctor writes a prescription and hands it to Monique.

"Get the prescription filled, take the pills and call my office for an appointment in two weeks." The Doctor walks out. Sandra gets up and starts to dress. Monique helps her. "What's going to happen to me next?" Sandra moans. "Hopefully nothing." Monique laughs. "Is this what they call the aging process?" "If so, I can wait for it to hit me." "You're perfectly healthy," Sandra claims. "I'll get dressed, you can go get the car, I'll meet you downstairs at the entrance."

Spencer is waiting at the front door of the apartment for Sandra. He sees them coming and runs out to the parking lot. He opens the door for Sandra and helps her out of the car. "Monique called me and told me what happened." Monique drives off. In the apartment, Sandra looks around and can't believe her eyes. The living room, dining area, bathroom and kitchen are neat and tidy. The bed in the bedroom is made with the six pillows arranged neatly against the headboard. Hope goes up to Sandra and runs around her feet. Sandra picks her up. "How's my baby?" Hope licks her face and whines. "I missed you too. I missed both of you." Sandra kisses Spencer. "Things have sure changed here. I love you for putting everything in order. I'm certainly surprised." "I am trying to make you happy, like always," he smiles. I have to get to work. With my new show, I have three performances. You should get some rest, then maybe you and Monique can come to the midnight performance." "I'll call and see if she's available." Spencer picks up a back pack and goes out the door. Sandra lays down on the sofa.

Sandra and Monique sit at a front table at the *Mandarin*. A bell chimes twelve times. Then there is a drum roll. On stage, are four large gold poles from ceiling to floor with American flags at the top They surround a fifth pole in the center. On the opposite sides of the center pole, four scantily clad female strippers in red, white and blue sequined bras and panties slide down the poles. A spotlight shines on the fifth pole. The Announcer's voice blares through the speakers, "Ladies and Gentlemen for your pleasure, please welcome, "Mighty Ram. Spencer slowly slides down the center pole. A eye patch covers his left eye, a gold pirates cap is on his head. He wears a red, white and blue striped cape. He is dressed in red bikini underwear. His bare chest is sprayed with a red and blue valentine, the letters MR in white are in the center of the valentine. He circles around the pole to the music while the four stripper's wave small, American flags in each hand from the floor. The crowd applauds. Spencer continues moving to the music of a drum. He has that smug look on his face. He moves into the audience, and starts dancing around the tables closest to the stage. Women reach out and touch his arms and legs.

Sandra and Monique applaud. "Whoa, he gets better and better every time," Sandra yells to Monique. "It's those legs," Monique, states. "He told me his Mother said he would get involved with a leg woman. And that's about all I love about his body. I swear, I must be crazy." "I am tired Monique," says rising her arms over her head. "Me too," Sandra mimics.

Monique drops Sandra off at home. She walks inside, Hope runs to her, looking up and whining. Sandra picks her up. "Okay, baby, I'm home." Sandra sits on the sofa and places Hope next to her.

She takes her cell phone from her purse and dials Pedro's number. "Hey Pedro, I have a few bucks why don't you come and pick me up. Let's have a little fun. He's not around. He's working. A half hour? Okay, that's perfect."

Pedro picks Sandra up at her apartment and takes her to his apartment. Once inside the apartment, he leads her into his bedroom. They sit on the side of the bed. "Let me take a hit first," Sandra says as Pedro takes an envelope from his shirt pocket. She pulls out her stem and lays a rock of cocaine on top of it as Pedro takes off his clothes. She lights a rock lays the stem on the side table and lays back on the bed. Pedro unbuttons her shirt, and kisses her nipples, Lying beside her, he implores her to,"touch it, kiss it," pointing to his penis. Sandra is extremely accommodating, bringing loud groans from Pedro. "That's it baby. You got me going again. You know what to do. Don't stop." Sandra continues and brings Pedro to a devastating, moaning, smiling, climax. He bounces back against the pillow, shaking his body back and forth. "Whoa, Sandra you're the best woman I've ever had." "Was it better than the last time"? "It gets better and better all the time." Good, now let me have another hit." "My pleasure, sunshine." Pedro gives her a rock, she puts it on her stem and he lights it for her. "Well, it is time to go," Sandra says. "Need to get home before Spencer." "You still with that creep?" "For the time being."

Pedro drives Sandra home. She kisses him and goes to her apartment. Inside, she goes to the bathroom and turns on the shower. She plays with Hope while the water gets hot. When the shower is ready, she steps inside and scrubs her body with a brush. The shower door opens as she shampoos her hair. Spencer steps inside. Sandra smiles and washes his back. He turns around and kisses her. He pushes her against the shower wall and she lifts up one leg. They have hot, steamy sex, get out of the shower and rub each other dry with towels.

The next morning, Monique and Sandra sit in the conference room at Thomas' office. They're discussing their accounts. Sandra takes a puff from her inhaler and lights a cigarette. "I know the Duffy Brothers like that 10% discount so they'll stick with us." Sandra says. "Now if we can only get Mr. Brill to come aboard we can concentrate on building those two accounts in order to generate more business. Networking is very important in this situation." "You're right about that," Monique agrees. "So, it's time to start thinking abut designing our own brochure," Sandra goes on. "That's not hard to do." "And we still have to come up with a slogan for the Brill brochure," Monique says. "I've been thinking about that." Sandra says. "How about "We're the best…get rid of the rest. Using a 36 point Algerian font. Then at the bottom of the page, below the photograph "Serving our customers for over twenty years." "Sounds good". Monique agrees. Thomas is going back to Vancouver tonight. I promised I'd have lunch with him at *Gigolo's*. I'll discuss our ideas with him." "Is lunch all you're having?" Monique asks. "Probably not." Sandra picks up her purse and leaves.

Sandra and Thomas are at *Gigolo's* having lunch. Now Sandra, I'll be gone for at least eight weeks. I worked many years with Eugene. He really was my Tutor," Sandra says defensively. "You know very well what I'm talking about." Okay, Thomas, I am a grown woman who sometimes has stong-willed ways. But, somehow I always come through. Don't forget I am a widow with a purpose. Ivory Advertising has a reputation. I won't ruin that or have you lose money on us. What do you think about our ideas for the Brill brochure?" "I like your idea, very creative. But, what about the contract?" "I will call him in a few days. He'll said yes." You think you're that good, huh? "I know we're that good. Now, order me another ginger ale." "That's my girl. Now you're talking," Thomas says proudly. "Want to come to my place?" "If you're a good boy," Sandra answers.

In Thomas' penthouse, Sandra walks to the kitchen opens the refrigerator door and takes out a bottle of water. He comes to the kitchen in his boxer shorts. Sandra takes a swig of the water. "Getting ready for me?" Thomas asks. "I'll meet you in the bedroom, darling." Thomas walks away. Sandra goes to the living room and retrieves her inhaler from her purse, takes a puff then takes out a pill bottle and swallows a pill. "Don't want to have a seizure on the man," she says to herself. She removes her dress, keeps on her bra and panties and high heels.

She struts into Thomas' bedroom. He's laying on the bed. Jazz music is playing, Sandra starts an erotic dance and motions for Thomas to join her. He gets up and they dance. His erection is so hard that his shorts are bulging. "You sure know how to get a man going." "Are you ready for your ultimate sexual experience?" "I told you once and I'll tell you again, I am not interested in any man's penis in my backside."

They fall back on the bed. "My cock is so hard my underwear hurts." He removes his boxer shorts. Sandra takes off her bra and panties. Thomas jumps on top of Sandra. She holds her legs up in the air, and wraps them around his neck. She still has on her stiletto heels. He enters his hard penis inside her. She moans while he thrushes in and out of her. Thomas keeps going as Sandra pleas, "slow down enjoy the moment." Thomas takes his time with having a climax. "Squeeze my balls," he orders Sandra. "You know I can't reach them," she moans. Thomas removes his penis lays back on the bed and starts to masturbate. "Squeeze my balls now," he orders. Sandra does what he asks. He let's out a loud groan and has a organism. The come shoots out on his hand. Sandra gets up, goes to the bathroom and comes back with a wet washcloth. "Have you ever had a threesome?" "No," Sandra lies. "I mean you me and another man." "Sounds like double trouble to me," Sandra laughs.

"I'll always have a hard on for you, Sandra. Have had one ever since I met you." Even when Eugene was alive?" "Yes, But I always kept it to myself." "You certainly did. I had no idea." Sandra hears her phone ringing from her purse in the living room. "I better get that, it could be Monique." She rushes into the living room. "Ivory Advertising," "Hello Mr. Brill, I m fine How are you? You will? Yes, we'll see you at your office tomorrow morning at nine. Sandra runs in the bedroom. She runs to the bed and jumps for joy forgetting she has on her heels. She falls down and hits her head on the bedside table. Blood streams down her face. "What the hell," Thomas says as he bends over her. "Don't worry," she assures him still smiling. "I m okay."

She gets up and walks into the bathroom and looks in the mirror. She takes a towel and dabs the blood from the cut on her forehead. Thomas stands behind her. They're both still naked. "Bad girl, who was on the phone?" Thomas asks. "That was Mr. Brill he's hiring us to design, produce and print the brochure for his company. I've never felt like this before, this is wonderful, what an accomplishment." "What about me? you got me at your beck and call don't you?" Thomas says as he wraps his arms around her and plays with her ample breasts. "You know as well as I do that you're a different kind of man in my life. You're special. He's business." "That's special too," Thomas says. "Come on I m just teasing you. I am proud of you and the entire team. One of the best investments of my life. Thank God. I can't lose you now. Let's get dressed and go to the office." Thomas asserts.

At the office, Sandra and Monique are dancing around the room hugging each other like little girls. "We have to stop playing around and get ourselves in order for the appointment," Sandra smiles. "Frank needs to add the suggested slogan to the layout. Are we going to stick with, We're The Best Get Rid Of The Rest?" "For the time being. When we tell him what we suggest he may come up with a better idea." "Let's not forget to take the invoice for the security fee of a thousand dollars. My Landlord is patiently waiting." Sandra says. "And I still will loan you the four hundred." Monique adds. Thomas walks in. "Well, girls you about ready for your morning appointment?" "More than ready."

"Sorry I have to leave tonight. But, I know you'll call me with all the details." "You bet we will," Monique says proudly.

The next morning, Sandra and Monique drive in to the parking lot of the Brill Company building. They walk inside the Waiting Room and announce themselves. The Receptionist tells them that Mr. Brill had a stroke last night and is in the hospital. There is no word as to when he will be back in the office. The women look at each other in disappointment and confusion. They walk back to the car in distress, "What am I going to do?" Sandra wails. "Let's go to my place," Monique offers. "I'll fix us breakfast. Then we can go to the office."

In Monique's apartment, the women sit at the kitchen table. Bacon is frying in a skillet on the stove. "How do you like your eggs?" "Over easy," Sandra answers. "I've been thinking," Monique says. "I have a saving account. So, I can loan you all the money for your rent." "You'd do that for me?" "Why?" "Because I love you." "Like a sister, right?" "No, wrong, more than that." "I'd like for you to be my significant other." "You mean like a same sex relationship?" "Something like that." "I promise to love you faithfully. You're all I need." "Breakfast is ready." They sit at the kitchen table and eat breakfast.

"I didn't know this about you, Monique. It is quite a surprise." "I thought after all these years, you'd think something was different about me. I have no boy friends in my life. That interlude with you and Eugene was all for you. You are my kind of woman, beautiful, intelligent and full of personality and energy. With me I think you could even stop drinking and drugging." "Yeah, those two years of sobriety, then I sure went down the drain." Now, I have 6 months. "We better get back to the office," Sandra says. "We're off whenever you're ready." Sandra takes a puff from her inhaler, picks up her purse and heads for the door. Once in Monique's car they hug long and firm. Monique kisses Sandra's hand.

The women walk into the conference room. They sit at the desk and open mail. "Because of you, Sandra," Monique offers, "I know what I want to do to help me settle down in life. I can dedicate my modeling career to Ivory Advertising. Become the Spokes Model for the agency to help bring in more business, Here is a check for fourteen hundred dollars to pay your rent." "Thank you for everything. I'll pay you back as soon as I can." Sandra smiles. "It's all for you my darling." "I don't feel well today, will you take me to the bank so I can deposit the check and then take me home?" Sandra asks. "Sure I will."

Sandra is on the telephone in her apartment, it is back in the same messy condition it was a few weeks ago. Spencer is asleep on the recliner. On television is the Stock Market channel. "Yes Mrs. Howard, you can pick up the check this evening. Around eight is fine." Sandra hangs up the phone gets a garbage bag and starts picking up old newspapers, magazines and Hope's soiled puppy pads. Then she empties the garbage cans making as much noise as she can to wake up Spencer.

He finally wakes up. "Would you help me get this place straightened up?" Sandra says in anger. "Mrs. Howard will be here at eight o'clock to pick up the rent check. And why do you have that channel on the television? You never play the stock market and unless I am wrong, you don't have any bonds either. Turn the radio on let's hear some good music." Spencer turns on the radio to a smooth listening station, gets the broom and starts to sweep the floor. Sandra takes a puff from her inhaler.

There is a knock on the apartment door. Sandra opens it for the Landlord, Mrs. Howard. "Here's the check Mrs. Howard. "Thank you for your patience." Mrs. Howard, a lady in her 60's takes the check and waves good-bye. Spencer waits for Sandra in the bedroom. Sandra calls out, "Spencer come in here." There is no answer. "Spencer?" Still no answer. Sandra walks into the bedroom. Spencer is laying on the bed snoring loudly. She shakes him awake. Spencer yawns, goes into the bathroom and turns on the shower. He sings in the shower. Sandra is totally appalled.

Sandra picks up the phone and dials Pedro's number. "Hi, I'm looking for Pedro. This is Sandra Walker, a good friend of his. You're his cousin? Okay. He's where? Oh my goodness. When did that happen? Last night? Okay, I'll call some other time." Sandra hangs up the phone and shakes her head in amazement. She dials Monique's number. "Hey, Monique, I just called Pedro, my contact, and his cousin told me he's in jail. Got picked up last night for possession. Why, don't you pick me up, we'll drop Spencer off at work and then go to the *Hideaway*, okay? Great, see you in half an hour."

At the *Hideaway*, Sandra checks out the room. She doesn't see anyone that she can ask about buying drugs. Monique orders a draft beer from the bartender and Sandra orders a ginger ale."Have you thought about what I told you?" "Not really, Monique answers. But, you should stop thinking about your addictions. We have a lot of work to do." "You're right. It's all because of Spencer. He's driving me crazy. Yesterday he was sitting on the toilet eating a peanut butter and jelly sandwich." "That's disgusting." "You bet it is." "I can't understand why he has such a lack of self-esteem. When I asked why he was doing that. He said he was hungry." " I think it's time you get away from him." "He's not helping you grow professionally or mentally." "All he keeps telling me is how much he is in love with me. He doesn't understand his way of loving is only coming from his heart not from his actions. I have a plan to get rid of him. I can't instigate it until we get the business going." Tell me about it when we're in a quieter place. I can hardly hear you in here."

"You know, I really appreciate Thomas," Monique says. "So do I." "I have very serious feelings about him." "I know you do." "My next step with him, is to stay as close as I can." "He's very, very special. However, I feel a little guilty because of his past with Eugene. "I believe Eugene would be happy for both of you. Even though Thomas was his best friend. Wait and see what happens. Don't push it." "I just can't wait to get rid of Spencer the slob."I can't stand his farting all the time. In bed, in the kitchen, everywhere in the apartment. "When you live with someone like that pretty soon you start picking up their bad habits." "You're right," Monique agrees. "His actions are so stupid that I don't even want to have sex with him as he calls it. Besides, I rather make love to my significant other, which should be him, instead of making an appointment to watch him masturbate. Monique laughs, "Let's go to the *Mandarin* and see how Mighty Ram is doing." "Okay, you've got a deal." Sandra laughs."He probably farts while sliding down the pole." "You're right about that, "Monique gushes.

At the *Mandarin*, Sandra and Monique sit as far away from the stage as possible. They don't want Spencer to know of their presence. The show is just beginning. The bell chimes twelve times. Then there is a drum roll. On stage, are the four large gold poles from ceiling to floor with American flags at the top They surround a fifth pole in the center. On the opposite sides of the center pole, four scantily clad female strippers in red, white and blue sequined bras and panties slide down the poles. A spotlight shines on the fifth pole. The Announcer's voice blares through the speakers, "Ladies and Gentlemen for your pleasure, please welcome, Mighty Ram. Spencer slowly slides down the center pole. A eye patch covers his left eye, a gold pirates cap is on his head. He wears a red, white and blue striped cape. He is dressed in red bikini underwear. His bare chest is sprayed with a red and blue valentine, the letters MR in white are in the center of the valentine. He circles around the pole to the music while the four stripper's wave small, American flags in each hand. The crowd applauds. Spencer continues moving to the music of a drum. He has that smug look on his face. He moves into the audience, and starts dancing around the tables closest to the stage. Women reach out and touch his arms and legs.

The difference about this show is that Spencer returns to the stage. The female strippers place their flags in a circle on the floor around him and then surround him and he slowly removes their bras and panties. After they are naked they dance around him and remove his cape. The music changes to upbeat, smooth music. Spencer licks his tongue around his upper lip. The crowd yells, "Do it…do it." The strippers take off his shorts which reveal a red, white and blue jock strap. Monique and Sandra look at each other in astonishment, then laugh. The crowd goes wild. Sandra points to the exit door. Monique nods her head. They get up, weave through the crowd and leave.

At Monique's apartment, the women share a joint in the bedroom. Sandra blows out the smoke and starts coughing and choking. "Are you alright.?" Monique asks. Sandra shakes her head no while she continues to choke. "Should I call 911?" "No I'll be fine in a minute. I need to cough up the mucus." She goes on choking and wheezing. Monique puts her arm around her shoulder. Sandra throws up the mucus. Monique guides her to the bathroom. Sandra kneels in front of the toilet. She looks at Monique. "It's almost over she gasps." Sandra throws up again.

Monique leaves and comes back with a glass of water. Sandra sits on the toilet seat and takes a sip. How long has this been going on? That was the first time. "Don't worry I'll talk to my Doctor about it." "You better. There are too many people depending on you." "I know," Sandra responds." So, let's get some rest and get ready for tomorrow. I'll give you a massage to help calm you down." Monique let me tell you something, love is such a beautiful game. But, I don't want to play it with you. Monique shrugs her shoulders gets undressed and goes to bed.

The next morning, at the office, Sandra is talking on the phone. "Thomas, I don't want to drink or do drugs again, my sobriety is very important to me. I'll make you proud of me, I promise. I'd love to have dinner with you when you get back to town. But eight weeks is so long. Can't you come back sooner?" "I can wait two more weeks. I think about you everyday. You do?" "I'm ready. Sandra hangs up the phone with a big smile on her face. Monique walks into the room. "I just talked to Thomas. He wants to have dinner with me again." "I don't blame him." "Let's go to the *Gigolo* and plan our future, Sandra suggests. "Great idea. I m ready. And I m hungry." The women collect their portfolios and brief cases and walk out.

At the *Gigolo*, they sit at a table on the outdoor patio having Cobb salads for lunch. Monique has her beer and Sandra has ginger ale. "So with Duffy Brothers we could possibly get the start up cash from them for their project. Mr. Duffy is ready to rock and roll. We need to sit down with Frank and discuss the layout and the characters in the book. Then George will choose the newspaper print. We have to come up with a storyline every month." Which will have to be approved by the client, Monique adds.

"Sandra, I want you to understand how I feel about you. It's extremely serious." I know, you told me that before. It's a bit confusing because we're working together and you're what I thought was and is my best friend. And that's without a same sex relationship. But, I have to tell you the offer is interesting. I like the idea because of my need to get away from Spencer as soon as possible. Besides a slob, he's spoiling Hope to no end." "What's he doing, now?" He feeds her by hand. He has 5 different food bowls on the floor in the kitchen. Then he'll feed Hope all her food, which could be whatever he's eating, from the palm of his hand. This morning he was sitting on the sofa eating cereal from a bowl and dropping milk soaked pieces on the sofa for Hope." "Are you telling him how you feel?" "Everyday. Enough, is enough. And I am sick and tired of his sloppy ways. It's hard to stay sober around him. He keeps telling me everyday that he's going to change." "He'll never change. He is too old. You're looking for a miracle," Monique moans. If you move in with me we can walk Hope on the beach. And you'll have your own bedroom. My condo is your home." "Well, I definitely need a change.

"Hey, I've got an idea." "What's that?" Sandra asks. "Let's go pick up Hope, take our laptops and go to the beach. We can work on the storylines on our laptops while Hope plays in the sand." They go to Sandra's apartment. Monique waits in the car. Sandra puts Hope's leash and collar on and walk her to the car. Okay, let's go we're ready. They drive to the beach.

At the beach, they discuss nearly a dozen storylines within an hour which would fit the layout of the book every month. Sandra is thrilled with their creative energy. Monique smiles with pride of the likelihood that they will have clients sooner than they thought. "Now that we know how well we can work together, let's talk about our personal future," Monique requests. "What are you suggesting?" I love you Sandra. You know that." "Yes, I do. But, so do several other people and they're men." "Don't joke with me. You don't need Spencer in your life and you're just playing a game with Thomas." "You're wrong about Thomas. I have true feelings for him and he feels the same way about me." "You just think he does. Has he told you how he feels?" "To some degree he has." "Like what?" "I'd rather not discuss how we feel about each other." "You're saying that to me your best friend?" "Being a best friend doesn't mean you have to share everything with each other." "I guess you're right. But I thought differently." Sandra's phone rings. She answers it. "Hi Thomas. Monique and I are working at the beach." "I thought it was time to take Hope out for some sun and sand. You're in town. Marvelous. Of course I can see you tonight. Pick me up at 7 I'll be ready." Sandra looks at Monique with a wide grin spread across her face. "So the King is coming to get the Queen," Monique teases.

Sandra sits on the sofa in her apartment. Hope lays by her side. There's a knock on the door. Sandra opens it and Thomas is there holding a bouquet of roses. They kiss, he hands her the flowers, takes her arm and they walk out the door.

At the *Gigilo* they sit at a candlelit table. Thomas is holding Sandra's hand. Romantic music is playing in the background. Thomas whispers in Sandra's ear. "I've changed my mind about never wanting to marry again. I want you to be my one and only for the rest of our lives." "I accept your offer," Sandra smiles. Thomas gets up and holds out his hand. "Shall we dance?" "By all means."

The next morning, Sandra and Monique are sitting at the conference table at the Ivory Advertising office. Sandra is beaming, glowing. "I can't believe he really wants me to be his wife after being single all these years." "Wake up girlfriend. He loves you," Monique retorts. "I haven't felt love like this since Eugene." "Of course not, it's a different kind of love." "He didn't even mention my addiction." "You mean addictions." "Come on are you my sister or what?" "Just don't want you to make a mess of your new coming of life." "You have to help me." "You know I will." "Your first step is to find a fellowship close to your apartment and start going to the meetings." "You're right. He didn't even say when we should get married." "Ask him." "I will. But first I have to talk to Spencer. He can keep the apartment. We can stay friends. We don't have sex anymore anyway."

Thomas walks into the room. "Well my darlings what are we talking about?" "The fact that you and I are going to be husband and wife." Sandra smiles. "Monique would you let me talk to Sandra alone." "Of course." Thomas takes Sandra in his arms and kisses her passionately. "We have to plan this so everyone besides us is happy." "If we're happy they will be happy" "I just want you to stay sober and be the wife I've been looking for a woman like you all these years. It's time to stop falling through the cracks." They kneel on their knees in prayer.

Monique walks back into the room. "Well what do we have here a church service. "Monique Thomas asked me to marry him again" "My Lord what a surprise. The man must really be serious." Monique hugs Sandra and Thomas. "When is this major event going to happen?" "We haven't decided yet.""Let me know when you do I want to be the first to know," Don't worry you will," Sandra smiles. Thomas picks up his brief case. Well, ladies I have a important appointment. I'll meet you at the Giglio for dinner. He kisses Sandra hugs Monique and leaves. The women hug each other. They sit down at the conference table."I haven't told Thomas but my lower back is causing so much pain my doctor said I have to have a nerve block on both sides of my back." "No way." "It's an out patient procedure. But someone has to be with me." "You know I'll go with you." "Thank you." "I'll get it done when Thomas goes back to Canada.

In the meantime, let's get to work on the Brill account. Monique takes out the layout. The phone rings. "Sandra answers it, Ivory Advertising. This is Sandra. Where will I get a back brace and a cane? Why do I have to wear a brace? But I thought the nerve blocks would stop the pain. Okay, I'll be there tomorrow. Sandra hangs up the phone and starts crying." "They said I have to wear a back brace and use a cane until the nerve block procedure. I'm to vain for that. Monique hugs her. "I want to go home I need some rest." "I understand. Come on I'll take you."

In her apartment, Sandra takes off her brace and puts it in the closet with her cane she then sits in her favorite chair holding Hope. She talks out loud wondering why such negatives have to happen to her. She picks up her cell phone. "Hi is Pedro there? Hey Pedro. It's Sandra. Why didn't you call me to let me know you're out. I have stopped. But today, I need a little help with my nerves and anxiety. Come over and bring the usual. I have the money."

Pedro knocks on the door. Sandra opens it and is shocked beyond words. Pedro's head is shaved bald. He walks in and hugs Sandra. She is speechless. "I shaved my head in jail."" I don't like it." "You don't have to. I didn't do it for you." "And we have an attitude. Forget my order. I'm not going to start again," Pedro turns around with a huff and walks out the door. A few minutes there is another knock on the door. It's her neighbor, Nora. " Sandra, I made some brownies and thought you would like one. And I have a few dollars for some ciggies." Sandra takes the money and gives Nora the pack of cigarettes. "Here take them all I'm quitting today." Nora hugs Sandra and leaves. Sandra picks up the phone and calls her hairdresser. "Cindy can you do my hair today? Okay I'll be there by 3.

Sandra walks out of the beauty salon looking like a new woman. She is minus brace and cane. She hails a taxi and goes shopping in Beverly Hills. After a few stops and purchases at her favorite boutiques she sits outside at a popular local café and has a cup of coffee. When she finishes her coffee she gets in a taxi and goes home.

Monique is setting in her car waiting to see the new Sandra. Sandra walks up to the car and knocks on the window. Monique jumps back and laughs. "Girl, look at you." "Yeah, I was tired of my hair. Think Thomas will like it?" "Hell yes. He'd be crazy if he doesn't. "I saw a few dresses that could be my wedding dress. But, I have to tell you my health is causing me worry. COPD is incurable and my lower back is getting worse." Come on lets go to the Hideaway for a ginger ale and we'll talk about aches and pains.

At the Hideaway, the women sit at the bar sipping soft drinks. "If Thomas truly loves you he'll help you get through all your problems." Monique claims. "He acts like it." "Here, lets make a plan." "Okay." "While Thomas is in Canada, we'll get the nerve blocks done in your lower back. It's not a big deal. It's all an out patient procedure. Call the doctor's office now and make the appointment. Sandra takes out her phone and dials the number. She makes the arrangements while Monique plays the jukebox. She puts the phone away and orders another ginger ale. Monique comes back to the bar. "So, what happened?" "I'll have the nerve blocks next Wednesday. "A week from today." Sandra responds. "Now we should find meetings for COPD victims. We can look them up on the computer. But you know Sandra you have to stop smoking."

Sandra smiles and sticks her tongue out. "Don't act like a child. Smoking can kill you." "Like I don't know it. I know this woman who walks around carrying her inhaler every where she goes. And she smokes a pack a day." "So do you." "Look bitch, don't start judging me. I gave my last pack of cigarettes to my neighbor. So I'm way ahead of you." "I'm so proud of you," Monique smiles. I think it's important that Thomas knows about your plans." "I don't." Sandra's phone rings. She answers it. "Hi Sweetheart. I'm fine. How are you? You're coming back tonight? You miss me that much? I'm honored. You want me and Monique to pick you up at the airport? I know your car is at the condo garage. See you tonight. Love you too. "That was Thomas." "So I heard." "We're picking him up at the airport."

The threesome sit at a table at Giglio's. Thomas takes a small box out of his pocket. He takes Sandra's hand."My darling, I ask for your hand in marriage. Will you marry me?" Monique and Sandra smile like teenagers. "Yes my dear, I'll marry you." Thomas puts a 2 carat diamond on Sandra's finger. They kiss and hold each other in their arms.

About the Author

Gwendolyn Bernhard started her writing career in Hollywood, California. She wrote stage plays and musicals. She was also married to Manfred Bernhard the creator of Big Boy, the icon for Big Boy Restaurants of America. They published The Adventures of Big Boy during a 25-year period. The book was a 16 page, four-color comic book for the children who ate at the restaurants with their families. Gwendolyn handled the membership club by organizing and mailing out the membership kit.

While living in Hollywood, Gwendolyn appeared in major motion pictures and numerous television commercials and print ads. Throughout the years, Gwendolyn has learned from a life long study how to bring to light the spiritualization and inspiration of the basics of life.